2014 W

Royal Palm Literary Awards

Unpublished Women's Fiction Category

Kathy

Merciful Blessings

by

N.L. Quatrano and D.K. Ludas

N.L. Quatrano

Published 2018 by Two Stone Lions Press
Printed in the United States of America
ISBN 13: 978-1-62390-075-5
E-ISBN: 978-1-62390-076-2

Photography by Alessandro Graziano.

For information, address:
Two Stone Lions Press
1202 Old Agateville Road
Hillsboro GA 31038

Two Stone Lions Press is a division of Salt Run Publishing LLC

Dear Readers,

We love you. We love life. We love the Lord. And we love being able to write stories about ordinary people up against extraordinary circumstances and being led to prevail. People just like you and us.

We're all a little bit broken, you know? Life does that to us. The nice thing about recognizing that we're all in the same boat to some degree is that we don't need to judge folks, but can observe, learn, maybe pray for them, and move on to what is ours to do. And in our case, take notes and turn them into fictional characters in our books.

Both of us are busy ladies. We have husbands who expect clean houses, stocked refrigerators, and assistance with outdoor chores. We're independently employed in addition to our writing. We do a lot of community things because we both feel it's important to contribute to the communities we live in and organizations we belong to. Now past retirement age, we spend a little more time visiting doctors for ourselves or our spouses.

Many of you have full plates too, and we thank you for taking your time and money to buy and read this book. We hope you'll enjoy meeting and following the Blessing sisters as much as we did while we traveled through the story-building process. Won't you please drop us a line and let us know what you think? Tell us what you think Faith, Grace, and Hope should get into next. We'd love to hear from you. We might even send you a little thank you gift, you never know!

Maybe we'll get to meet at a book signing someday and if so, please introduce yourself. We look forward to meeting you–or hearing from you–soon.

We both wish you blessings galore!

D. K. Ludas *N. L. Quatrano*

D. K. Ludas N. L. Quatrano

D.K Ludas & N.L. Quatrano

D.K. Ludas and N.L. Quatrano are experienced short mystery story writers. They've been friends a good long time, too. Well, more like sisters than friends, really. They've been in Romance Writers of America and Sisters in Crime and Mystery Writers. They're still with Sisters in Crime. Ludas in Central New Jersey and Quatrano in Northeast Florida.

When they first brainstormed this series, they just loved the idea that smart, independent women of faith could have their ups and downs, face their demons, find their common bond and then band together to defeat their enemy.

About the only thing more important to both writers than families and friendship is their faith in the Lord. It is central in their lives. They glorify Him for the fever He instilled in them to write, the guidance to write what will serve Him, and their relationship with each other.

It is their prayer that you'll be entertained and encouraged by the Amazing Grace Series. Both ladies enjoy hearing from readers, and would love to know what you thought of this book.

Dedications

I dedicate this book to the women in the world who keep things running from their homes, their businesses, and their hearts, no matter what they are facing. My co-author Daria is one of those amazing women and I consider myself blessed to call her my friend.
~N.L. Quatrano

I dedicate this book to all sisters who have faced problems in their lives, and bonded together to resolve them. My co-author, Nancy, is my "shero" and my inspiration. Working together we can "move mountains."
~D.K. Ludas

Contents

About The Authors

Trust in the Lord with all your heart,
On your own intelligence rely not;
In all your ways be mindful of Him,
He will make straight your paths.
Proverbs 3:5-6

Chapter One

Hope

Percival Blessing was at peace. Head down on his desk, his right cheek resting on the morning paper, his arms dangled loosely at his sides.

But it wasn't morning. And Percy, as he was known to family and friends, wasn't sleeping. On his seventy-eighth birthday, he'd gone home to his beloved Elizabeth.

"Oh, Daddy," Hope sobbed as she clutched the doorframe of his study, "if you didn't want to join me for your birthday, all you had to do was say so."

The old farmhouse creaked around her as if to agree it too would miss the old trucker. She dragged herself to his desk and stroked his head as tears splashed onto her fingers and into the gray hair beneath them.

In the quiet she could hear the ticking of the grandfather clock that stood in the hallway, an anniversary gift from her father to her mother, a woman gone since Hope was eighteen.

"Give Mom my love, Daddy. I will miss you so much."

She swiped the tears off her face with her sleeve and with a heavy sigh, she moved into the hallway, picked up the telephone, and dialed 911.

Up to her neck in vanilla-scented bubbles, something she'd remembered to bring to the farmhouse from home, Hope took a sip of red wine, rested her head against the tub, and let the warm water relax overworked muscles. It had been a long day of cleaning and polishing the old farmhouse, but one she'd found comforting in many ways.

She smiled with the memory of her younger sisters, ignoring momentarily the fact that a chasm the size of the Grand Canyon seemed to stand between her and them. She remembered Grace standing in the dining room with her fists resting on skinny hips, always ready for a fight.

Then, her thoughts drifted to Faith. It would be so great to see her gentle sister again. Unwrapping and putting out the doll collection Faith so cherished as a child sparked memories of the hours Faith spent in her room dressing and undressing them. Though twins, Faith and Grace were as different in most ways as night was to day.

Hope finally emerged from the large claw-footed tub, almost too tired to stand on her feet, slipped into her nightshirt, shut off the bathroom lights, and took her wine glass down to the kitchen.

After she double checked the locks on the front and back doors, she headed upstairs to bed. As she closed the door to her room, the clock chimed nine times.

She knelt beside her bed and bowed her head. "Lord, thank you for a safe journey home for Faith and Grace. And please let us become a loving family again."

Smash! Thud.

Hope bolted upright in bed. *What the hell was that?* Barefooted, she tiptoed to the landing and looked downstairs. The front door was still closed and locked. *Maybe I was dreaming . . . .*

She turned to climb back in bed when she heard the long, mournful creek of the middle drawer of her father's desk.

Holy Moses! Someone's in the house.

Her heart pounded as she fought for a deep breath. Sheer panic kept her feet planted firmly on the floor, despite the fact she knew she had to move.

Slam!

The loud noise from the floor below jolted her into action and she scurried into her father's room and quietly locked the door. Gasping for air, fingers trembling, she reached for the telephone on the nightstand and for the second time in three days, dialed 911.

The dispatcher answered on the third ring.

"Someone's broken into my house," Hope whispered. She glanced nervously at the bedroom door and clutched the phone in a death grip to keep from dropping it. She concentrated on answering the man's questions.

"I'm locked in the upstairs bedroom. I can hear someone downstairs. Sounds like they're in my father's office."

He asked where her father was.

"He died two days ago. I'm alone here tonight."

A moment, then another question.

"No, I don't have a gun," Hope almost yelled. *If I had a gun, I wouldn't be talking to you.*

She looked around the room and focused on one of the windows.

"Okay, I can get out the window, I think. There should be a fire ladder in the closet. I'll figure out something. Please, just hurry."

Hope could hear the dispatcher speak to someone else. The "second" he asked her to hold the line felt like a year. Then he was back. A patrol car was on the way.

Hope placed the phone into the cradle and tiptoed to the closet. After shuffling through her father's clothes, she found the green neon ladder where it had always been.

She took it to the window and gripped the sash to lift, hoping it wouldn't make enough noise to betray her. Biting her lip, she moved the window upward ever so slowly.

Crash! That sounded like it had come from the living room.

Dear Lord, she hoped it wasn't the Waterford crystal vase Daddy had given Mother for their tenth anniversary. This intruder was violating her family. She ground her teeth and clenched her fists.

Despite the fear-induced nausea that threatened to choke her, she marched over to the door and released the tiny thumb latch. *They have no right!* She heard more crashing downstairs. *What if they have guns?*

She stopped, took a deep breath to try and relax the tightness in her chest. She rested her head against the door and reset the lock. *Grace and Faith don't need two funerals to attend . . . .*

She ran to the window and dropped the fire ladder outside. Carefully, she felt for the first step with her bare toes, then climbed down in the dark as fast as she could.

Red and blue flashing lights danced in the palm trees by the garage as she made her way down the side of the house. She jumped the last two feet to the ground and jogged toward the Sheriff's vehicles.

She rounded the house in time to see two deputies pull their guns out and crash through the front door. *Something else to fix.* Huddled beside their cars, she wished she had on more than her "Redneck Woman" nightshirt. Her feet were wet with the dew on the grass and way too much leg was exposed for a woman of AARP age.

Within minutes, the officers escorted the intruder out of the house in handcuffs. Hope began to walk toward them, then stopped in disbelief. Her fear turned to anger so hot she was speechless. She broke into a run, bare feet forgotten.

"How dare you?" she screamed, just as a deputy grabbed her by the arm to stop her charge.

"What are *you* doing here?" the prisoner snarled.

"*Me*? What am *I* doing here? I was born here, raised here. This is my father's house. I *belong* here," Hope replied.

"Not any more, you don't, Missy. See you in court."

The intruder was none other than Hope's long-time nemesis, Betty Jo Clark.

Chapter Two

Grace and Faith

Grace Blessing looked out the tiny aircraft window beside her seat as the plane taxied to the gate. Tall, royal palms swayed in a steady breeze, but didn't look all that much different from those she'd left behind in Israel. She wiped a hand across her eyes. She felt like the oldest forty-six-year-old on the planet.

When her sister Hope had called her three days ago about their father's sudden death, she'd stowed the pain, made arrangements with her commanding officer for a ten-day leave, and packed her dress blue uniform and two civilian outfits. She'd flown in her army greens and toted her duffle bag, slightly surprised at the salutes and smiles she received at every airport from Tel Aviv to Jacksonville, Florida. It seemed that even the Army Corps of Engineers was in favor since the United States had declared war on terrorism.

When the pilot announced that they could begin to disembark, her stomach flipped. Three days ago, it seemed she had forever to figure out what to say to her older sister Hope, and now she would see her in less than an hour and she had no clue. After more than fifteen hours of flying, she was almost too tired to worry about it.

Why had they drifted so far apart the past twenty years? Grace knew that when she'd left Blessing Farm she wouldn't return there to live, but she wasn't sure any more why she had so much animosity for her sister. Hope had done her best to raise two younger sisters after their mother died of cancer.

Grace sighed and signaled the couple across the aisle from her to go ahead. At five-feet-eleven-inches tall, she was used to ducking to avoid head injuries in small places, but it took a little additional time to wrangle her duffle out of the overhead compartment. Without making eye contact with anyone, she filed out of the plane, walked up the jet way, and took a seat in the spacious waiting area in the Jacksonville International airport to wait for her sister.

Faith, her younger twin by eleven minutes, was due in on the five-fifteen from Dallas/ Fort Worth Airport. Grace glanced at the flight status board. *Forty minutes.* Time enough for a cup of coffee at the Starbucks across the courtyard.

Grace took her coffee and settled back into a rocking chair to wait. She smiled, thinking of the fun they'd had as kids growing up on the farm. Though they'd been as different as frogs and birds, they did share a bond that went beyond tomboy and princess. They'd often shared sorrows without words. Over the years they'd remained in contact with each other, even if they'd neglected Hope and their father.

It wasn't intentional, she thought. Their father had been closer to Hope than to his other two daughters, so they'd simply gone on about their lives, leaving him and Hope to carry on.

Or, maybe all of that was crap . . . .

Checking to make sure her bag was stowed beneath the rocker, Grace leaned back in the chair and closed her eyes. The flight had been long and the stop in Philadelphia International to get through customs had taken forever. She hadn't seen four good hours' sleep in as many days.

She needed to be strong. To bury her father. To visit with Faith. To face Hope.

She opened her eyes, drank the rest of her coffee, and checked her watch. *Twenty-five minutes to show time.*

Faith woke from an exhausted sleep when the flight attendant asked her to pull the seat-back upright. The delay out of Dallas/Ft. Worth had been three hours on top of the two hours she'd already been sitting there, thanks to the latest security threat. Four hours in the air and she was ready to stretch her legs for sure. She took the last swig of spring water from the bottle she'd tucked into the magazine pocket.

She released her thick, blonde hair from the clip at the nape of her neck. A tear rolled down her cheek as she ran her fingers over the ivory pelican and remembered how proud Daddy had been when he presented it to her at her high school graduation. *Daddy, I'm going to miss you so much.*

In fifteen minutes, she'd see her sisters Grace and Hope. She was excited to see Grace again, as they'd spent ten days together for Christmas two years ago, when tensions at the Gaza Strip had been so high that engineers had been sent stateside for some much-needed R&R. But she hadn't done much more than speak with Hope on the phone or via the occasional email in more than five years. *Maybe longer if I'm being honest.*

Faith swiped at another tear. *How can Daddy be dead? How could the God he taught us has so much love, just rip him out of our lives this way?*

She searched her jacket pocket for a tissue and blew her nose. She sighed. *Maybe God took him because we weren't appreciating him anymore.*

The plane touched down with a bump, and taxied to the gate. In ten minutes she'd be in the arms of her sisters. Sisters who both loved her in their own way. She'd do her best to make them happy in the few days she'd be here.

Then it was back home to Texas, her metalwork business, the chaos of two teenage sons, and her annoyingly immature ex-husband.

As Faith pulled her carry-on from the overhead near her seat, she glanced out the window at the bright, Florida sunshine and smiled. That dark hole of grief inside her brightened a little. Texas had a lot of fine things going for it, but Florida had the kind of sunshine that made a person smile, no matter what else was going on.

Like cattle heading to the livestock pens in Amarillo, the passengers made their way along the aisle, out the doorway of the plane, and up the jet way to the terminal. Faith's heart rate picked up with her pace. A few minutes' walk later, she spotted Grace standing near the rocking chairs at the end of the arrival tunnel.

"Hey, you! It's wonderful to see you," she said before she dropped her bag on the floor and stepped into Grace's outstretched arms.

"I know, me too," Grace murmured, patting Faith on the back. "Wish we'd just come home before Daddy died. This really sucks."

Faith straightened, tugged her red bolero jacket into place, and smoothed the lines from her black slacks.

"I know what you mean. That's all I could think about after I got Hope's call. Where has the time gone to?"

Grace shrugged. "Get your bag. If I know Hope, she's waiting for us downstairs at Baggage Claim. Ever practical, I'm sure she's already here."

Faith placed her hand on Grace's arm. "Are you worried about seeing her?"

Grace tilted her head to the side. "A bit anxious maybe. I'm ashamed that I may not even know who she is any more. I hope she's okay. This is probably going to be hardest on her since she was closest to Daddy."

Faith sighed and strode alongside her sister. "Yeah, that's

about how I feel, too. This time we can be there for her instead of the other way around, right?"

"Right. Like she'll let us contribute in any way . . . ."

"There's that, I suppose," muttered Faith.

Hope sat in her truck, so nervous that she was afraid she'd throw up her lunch.

After virtually no sleep, the day had started with a very early visit by the Alachua County Sheriff's Department for her statement regarding Betty Jo's break-in at the house. Then the insurance company had called about an overdue insurance payment for the farmhouse, and she'd had to transfer almost all of what was left of her meager savings into her checking account and quickly make the payment.

The accident on Interstate 75 had turned a two-hour drive into three, and she'd battled tears most of the way. Would she be able to keep her bitterness at bay? All the broken promises, and missed holidays, and now Daddy was gone. She knew she had to let it all go—it couldn't be undone. She prayed that her sisters wouldn't need much from her because she just didn't have much left to give anyone. Hope needed far more than she could give at this point.

She'd watched the arrival board from the waiting area. When Faith's plane showed up on the board arriving at the gate, Hope put her truck into Drive and made the loop to the arrival lane.

She sat curbside for all of two minutes when Grace's sleek, black and silver head appeared through the doors, with Faith a step behind her.

They look wonderful. Hope jumped out of the truck and pulled down the tailgate so they could stow their bags.

Faith threw herself into Hope's arms and sobbed. "I just can't believe he's gone."

Hope held her sister tight. "I can't believe he's gone, either. I don't know how I would cope if you two couldn't be here."

Grace cleared her throat. "We'd better get out of the traffic, or we'll have more funerals to deal with."

Hope smiled. Grace was always the pragmatic one. "You're right. Hop in, and we'll get out of here."

Faith climbed into the back seat while Grace pulled herself into the front passenger seat. Once everyone was belted in, Hope eased into the airport traffic and headed for I-295 westbound, toward home.

"Did you have good flights?" Hope asked, watching the side and rearview mirrors while she merged into the interstate traffic.

"The storm delays were annoying, but aside from that, trip was fine." Faith looked out the window. "It's warm here already, but sure is beautiful with the magnolias in bloom."

"Are the magnolias in Merciful blooming, too?" Grace asked.

"A few. Most of them are done already since the weather got warm so fast," Hope answered.

They drove for a time without speaking. Hope wondered if her sisters were as tired as she was, but less than ten miles from the airport, the answer was obvious. They were sound asleep.

She wondered if her sisters would notice the changes in the little town that had raised them. Main Avenue still sported shops on both sides of the oak-lined two-lane street. How would they react to the gigantic plastic cone now suspended above the ice cream parlor where they had spent so many of their afternoons as teenagers? And how would they feel about old man Strickler's General Store being closed? *No more penny candy barrels for little girls to rummage through.*

Well, after the funeral, there'd be plenty of time to show them around and find out how they felt about things.

Hope parked the truck in the Blessing Farm driveway. "Home, girls."

The familiar "home, girls" aroused Grace. How many times

during her high school years had Hope made that very same announcement after a late night at the football field or the movie theatre.

Grace sat up, unbuckled her seatbelt, and gazed at the huge Amazing Grace Trucking sign that hung above the garage bay doors. She relaxed against the headrest and grinned.

Amazing Grace Trucking. Her namesake. She recalled the first time she'd read her name on the sign. Her mother had them reading before they'd started kindergarten. One day, Grace and Faith had gone outside to play in the yard. They'd been playing with a ball when it bounced into the driveway down by truck garages.

Grace had looked up and read her name on the sign. She'd thrown the ball to Faith and run into the house as fast as her little legs could carry her. Breathlessly, she'd asked her mother why her name was on the building. She remembered how her mother had hugged her and explained how special her name was. "Grace" meant a "special blessing from God." Somehow, ever since her mother had died, she'd never really felt special again.

She leaned into the backseat and shook her sister. "Time to wake up, sleepyhead."

Faith stirred and sat up. 'Wow, did I sleep the entire way home from the airport?"

"You sure did," Grace said. "We both did."

"Let's go inside and get you settled." Hope opened the truck doors and walked around to drop the tailgate. "I knew you'd both be exhausted, especially you, Grace. I'll bet you feel like you've been on a plane forever."

Grace stretched her arms over her head and yawned. "You've got that right."

Luggage in tow, Grace and Faith went to the back-porch door, blazing ahead of Hope, whose arms were full of grocery bags. Grace held open the door.

Hope deposited the food goods on the kitchen counter.

"Welcome home, girls. Make yourselves comfortable. Everything seems to be pretty much in the same place it's always been."

Faith walked into the dining room and set her luggage down. She gazed around the room. She ran her fingers along the tapestry-covered chairs. *Oh, the nights Mom toiled endlessly sewing them.* Tears filled her eyes as she remembered helping her mother sort the colors and handing her the thread she needed.

Everything was just as it was when she left the farm for Texas all those years ago . . . except the two people who had been such a big part of her life were gone.

Assured that Hope didn't require any assistance, Grace climbed the stairs to her bedroom.

She tossed her duffle bag on the bed and looked around. The curtains were newer, but the quilt that her mother had lovingly sewn for her brought back bittersweet memories. The patches made from softened recycled flour sacks were unique and formed a center star pattern, even though it wasn't made for a full-sized bed.

How she'd fussed at her mother when it had appeared on her bed the first time. She didn't want the frills that Faith enjoyed, but she hadn't wanted this old thing, either. Now she ran her fingers along the hand stitched seams and fought back tears. Hell, now she'd dress in the damn flour sacks if it would bring back either of them.

She crossed the room and touched the 4-H trophy on the bookshelf. After her mother had died, Grace just about ate and slept 4-H. The summer of her seventeenth birthday, she'd won the prize for the best Florida Cracker cow in the competition. Unlike other kids who proceeded to put their prize-winning livestock up for auction, Grace had marched Pocahontas back on the trailer and Daddy had hauled the bovine back home to the pasture. He'd acted as though that was the only reasonable course of action.

In a shadow box she didn't remember, were her ribbons. Her father must have done that since her last visit. He'd been so proud of her, even when she hadn't brought home ribbons and trophies. I haven't been up here in a long time.

Her parents had taught her to care for other creatures, great and small. She sat on the edge of the bed. Maybe if she got honest about it, what they'd taught her was what led her to join the Army.

After all, she could see the world, and fix it, all at the same time.

Around nine o'clock Hope put three wine glasses on the kitchen counter and the block of cheddar cheese on the cutting board. She sliced the cheese and piled it in the center of a dish, then put Ritz crackers and Captain's Wafers all around the edge. A bottle of San Sebastian Red chilled in the fridge.

I hope they like wine and cheese. Sad that I don't even know if they'd have preferred beer, or something stronger.

She carried everything to the table on the screened porch. Tomorrow would be easier if they could share it as sisters. Hope said a prayer asking for peace and comfort for them all.

Hope stood at the base of the staircase and called to her sisters. Just like years ago when she'd called, they appeared in tandem at the railing on the landing. She pushed away the memories that tugged at her heart.

"I thought we could talk a little while. About tomorrow? I have some wine and cheese on the porch."

"Be right down." Faith turned toward the bathroom. "I need to take out my retainer, first."

"Aren't you a bit old for a retainer, kiddo?" teased Grace.

"Apparently not, since the dentist said I'll be wearing it until I die." Faith dashed out of sight. Grace descended the stairs.

"How you doing, Sis?" She followed Hope through the white

swinging door between the dining room and the kitchen.

Hope reached into the fridge for the bottle of wine. Grace picked up the corkscrew and took the bottle from her.

Hope leaned against the edge of the sink. "I'm still in shock, I think. Last week I called and asked him to dinner, next thing I know he's gone."

The cork pulled out of the bottle with a squeak. Placing the cork on the counter, Grace walked to the porch and poured them each a glass.

"You look like you're going to drop any minute. You getting any sleep at all?"

Hope shook her head. "We had a break-in here around midnight last night. That woke me out of a sound sleep. Then the sheriff was here at the crack of dawn to go over all the questions they asked me at two this morning. I feel like road kill."

Grace was on her feet. "A break-in? Did they catch anyone?"

Faith joined them in time to hear Grace's questions. "Who broke in where?"

Hope handed Faith her wine and motioned for them to sit down. "It was Betty Jo Clark. Should have seen her. Madder than a surprised skunk when they hauled her off in handcuffs."

Faith laughed first. The sound was like music to Hope's ears. She and Grace joined in and before long all three were laughing so hard tears streamed down their faces.

When they could talk again, Grace turned to Hope. "What was she looking for? Any idea?"

"None. Thought I'd look through the office when I got time, but today's been too busy. There was a small stack of mail from last week on Daddy's desk when I got here Monday, but I just locked it in his ledger drawer until we could go through it."

"She didn't talk to the law when they arrested her?" Faith snagged several crackers and a few slices of cheese.

"By her reaction it was clear she didn't realize I was staying here. After she told me this wasn't Daddy's house anymore, she asked for a lawyer, wouldn't say another word."

"Well, she's always been a bitch when it comes to you, Hope. But breaking in here seems a bit out of character even for BJ Clark." Grace ate a cracker. "You still keeping the business books these days?"

Hope smiled. "Nope. Got my own business to worry about. Daddy has, sorry, had a bookkeeper. She's been with him about five years, I think."

Faith cleared her throat. "I noticed the place is so overgrown it almost looks abandoned. Even mother's rose garden. Daddy was behind on things, I guess . . . ."

Hope tamped down the urge to snap at her sister. "My business is struggling, and I've been trying to help Daddy with money here and there, but I couldn't manage the farm, too. I locked up the shop and my apartment and came out here right after he died to get the house ready for you. It didn't look so bad a few weeks ago when I drove out to see him." Hope finished her wine and placed the glass on the table.

"Easy, Sis." Faith leaned forward and patted Hope's hand. "Not blaming you, just observing. Maybe we can help shape things up for you. Are you going to sell the place or stay here?"

Hope's eyes widened. "Gads, I haven't given it a thought. I'm sure Daddy left the place to all of us, which would be the only fair thing to do. He loved us all equally, you know that."

Grace grunted. "Not how I remember it, but it doesn't matter now. You stayed here and helped Father with everything, your whole life. You should get the farm."

"I don't want the farm. I want my sisters back in my life. I want him here to say dinner blessing. I want to go open my shop tomorrow morning and find out all this pain in my heart is just a bad dream." She swiped at an escaped tear. "I'm sorry."

Faith stood and crossed to the chair where Hope sat, and squatted in front of her older sister. Putting her arms around her, she held her close. "Nothing to apologize for."

Grace got to her feet and stood behind them. "It'll be okay,

Hope, you'll see. You get some sleep, and you'll feel like a new woman tomorrow."

Hope laughed and then pulled away from Faith's embrace, swiping her arm across her eyes. "You're probably right. I just wanted this to be as easy on you as possible, and here I am weeping like a fool."

"As always, you've gone above and beyond on our behalf," Grace said. "But we're all grown up now. You can't protect us from life's bruises any more. And maybe now we can help you with some of them."

Hope looked at the women before her. Grace was right. They were no longer the younger sisters that she had felt obsessively compelled to teach, train, and protect.

"I love you, you know," she whispered.

"We know. Now, tomorrow is the funeral. So, tell us what we need to know, and then we'd best get to bed. Yes?" The lieutenant colonel had spoken.

"Limo will pick us up here at ten; the service is at the church at eleven. After we lay Daddy to rest, we go back to the church for a fellowship lunch. We should be home near three, I guess."

"Okay, then. Let's say a prayer for a good night's sleep, and Daddy. Then off to our beds," offered Faith.

Sounds delightful to me. For the first time in her life, her sisters didn't need her—she needed them.

More than she'd ever dreamed.

Chapter Three

Snakes in the Grass

Inside the one-story Fellowship building, Hope sighed in relief as the cool air surrounded her. *Thank the Lord for air conditioning*. What a difference from the eighty-degree heat at the cemetery where they'd spent the last hour. A large-bosomed woman glided between the round white-clothed tables and then captured Hope in a hug.

"Does everything look all right, Miss Hope?"

Hope finally managed to extract herself and step back, a warm smile firmly in place. "Yes, Margaret Ann, it looks lovely. You ladies shouldn't have gone to so much trouble."

"Nonsense, your daddy gave us this church and you served us a good long while before Pastor Matt died."

Hope shrugged. "Ancient history now. But thank you so much for doing such a nice meal for us."

"You've done the same for us many times. The other ladies are in the kitchen. Smell that fried chicken? Your daddy's favorite."

"Probably what killed him," Faith hissed.

"Hush up!" Hope whispered. She glanced at Margaret Ann who seemed oblivious to the careless remark. These people, her friends, had made life easier for Hope, especially in the past five years. "I do smell it and it's wonderful. Cornbread, too?"

"Sure. Everything will be out as soon as the reverend gets here to say grace. Come have some punch and sit down with your sisters."

Armed with a glass of punch and a small plate of snacks, Hope and her sisters moved to the round table nearest the kitchen door.

"So, how's life since the divorce? The boys doing okay?" Grace faced Faith, determined to catch up on the lives of both her sisters even if she deplored small talk.

Faith shrugged, sipped her drink, and wrinkled her nose. "Better than it was when I was married. Much less stressful." She rubbed her temples with her fingertips. "By the way, isn't this retirement year for you? What are *your* plans, Colonel?"

Grace frowned but straightened her shoulders. "Lt. Colonel, actually. Maybe I won't retire. I'm only forty-six, I might stay another four years. Or maybe I'll join the Peace Corps."

Hope spewed her drink out all over the table. "What? When I wanted to do that, you thought it was the dumbest thing in the world." She grabbed a napkin, wiped her mouth, and blotted at the tablecloth.

"What the hell did I know? I was eighteen, you were the big-sister-know-it-all, and I thought *everything* you wanted was dumb." Grace picked up a sprig of green grapes and popped two into her mouth.

"Saint Hope! Always spending too much time trying to please everyone else. That's been your largest flaw, forever."

"I'm not a saint, Faith. I never tried to be one." Hope wiped the rest of the punch off the tablecloth with her napkin.

Lord knew, she made her fair share of mistakes along the way. She was only seventeen when she'd been forced into the role of motherhood for her twin sisters. Apparently, they still saw her as the evil older sister they'd left behind.

Faith motioned toward the door. The reverend had arrived, his light brown hair still disheveled by the breeze at the graveside, his starched white collar unbuttoned, black jacket thrown over his right shoulder. Perspiration marks showed on his shirt. Hope started to get up to greet him, but he waved her back to her seat.

"Thank God," said Grace. "Maybe now we can eat."

He made the blessing short, and in minutes huge aluminum pans of food were being consumed by the fifty or sixty people in attendance.

By two o'clock, only Hope, Grace, Faith, and four of the churchwomen remained. The hall had been cleaned and enough food to feed a platoon had been boxed to go to the farm. She'd insisted that the church women drop half of it off at the Goodwill kitchen on their way home.

The sisters sat silently drinking tall glasses of sweet tea, each dreading reentry into the heat.

The door creaked open and they looked up. Faith and Grace sucked in their breath and turned their attention toward their sister.

"Oh no, she's back," Hope croaked.

"That snake in the grass," hissed Faith out of the side of her mouth.

Betty Jo was still stunning to look at, even at fifty-five-years old, but she was mean as a coral snake and always had been. Her simple black sheath and white pearls went well with her slender build and carefully coifed artificially-blond hair. Hair that had been color-treated since she was thirteen and traveling the beauty pageant circuit. She glared in Hope's direction.

For a solid minute, the room was as quiet as a church waiting to hear the "I do's." Betty Jo waltzed past the church women without so much as a glance. She stopped less than two feet from Hope.

"You may think that you've won this round with me, but I assure you that I will be the winner in this game. When I find the original mortgage documents, and believe me, I will find them, I will toss you out on your ass once and for all."

Grace got out of her chair and joined Hope. "If we have to file a restraining order to keep you out of our way, we will. You're done harassing my sister. You can leave now."

Faith took up a position at Hope's other side. There was solidarity in the family, even if they had their differences. Betty Jo opened her mouth to speak, but apparently thought better of it. She shrugged indifferently, put her nose in the air, and turned to leave.

When Grace took a step toward their unwelcome guest, Hope put her hand out to stop her. The day certainly didn't need to end with a brawl. "Let it go. I don't know what she's talking about, but I'm sure come next week, she'll make it crystal clear."

"That woman has no shame. When in the world is she going to stop this senseless vendetta?" Faith said through clenched teeth.

Hope took a deep breath. She'd given up trying to make sense of it all on the day she'd buried Matthew, her husband of twenty years, who'd died of a heart attack in Betty Jo's four-poster bed. "Probably not until one of us is dead."

"I'm gonna lock that door," Margaret Ann said as she marched behind Betty Jo. She pulled back the drape on the window. "Lordy, I don't believe my eyes. One snake in the grass follows the other," she muttered.

"What's wrong now?" moaned Hope.

Before Margaret Ann could answer, the door opened.

"Oh my," Grace and Faith said in unison.

He approached the table, hands at his side, his stride unhurried. His light gray suit jacket was open to reveal only a little extra weight on his six-foot-tall frame. His brown eyes were friendly.

Eddie Highspring, former captain of the high school football team, stood tall as an oak tree a few feet from the table. "Hello, Hope."

What the hell! Was this suddenly Homecoming week and nobody'd told her? Hope couldn't breathe, let alone think straight. When the man-that-got-away cleared his throat, she finally blinked.

"Hello, Eddie. How've you been?" she managed to croak.

"Want me to throw *him* the hell out of here, too?" offered Grace.

Eddie raised his hands. "I came to offer my condolences to you all. Your father was a good man who loved you very much."

"Thank you," Hope said. "You didn't have to come all this way. A card would have been more than enough."

He shrugged, raising the shoulders of his Brooks Brothers jacket. "Ocala isn't all that far."

"Ocala?" Hope said, the color draining from her face like whitewash dripping down a fence on a southern summer day. Her hazel eyes narrowed to slits. "Ocala? How long have you lived in Ocala? I thought you were in Oklahoma or Idaho or Colorado or something."

He smiled, and she almost shivered. "I've been in Ocala almost twenty years."

"I see," Hope said.

"No, you don't. But this isn't the time or place to explain it."

Faith sprang from her chair. "Well, thanks for stopping by, Mr. Highspring. You can leave now, too. If you hurry, you can catch your ex-wife."

Grace stood also. "Hope, why don't we get going? Everyone's tired and we won't be in town all that long. We've got things to do."

Eddie slid his hands into his pockets. A sexy look, even for a man a couple of years shy of sixty. "I hope you're not leaving before the reading of the will."

"Don't care about the will. We're sure he left everything to Hope, anyway," Grace said. "Besides, how is that your business?" asked Faith.

"It's my business because your daddy made it my business. I'm your father's attorney and he made very specific bequests. You all need to be here for the reading of the will. It impacts you all."

Hope stood to join her sisters. "How long have you been Daddy's lawyer?"

He cocked his head to the side as though pondering the existence of the solar system. "About six months."

Hope clutched the edge of the table. *Damn.*

Faith and Grace exchanged a look and Margaret Ann gathered her friends and hightailed it to the kitchen where they could eavesdrop without being so obvious.

"Okay. If it's so important, we'll all be here. Let's read the will tomorrow. Get it over with," Grace said. Faith nodded. Hope stood as stiff as a concrete post.

"You sure that Hope can't just handle this?" Faith asked.

"I'm sure," said Eddie. "Meet me at your dad's place tomorrow afternoon. Will that work? I have a commitment in the morning, but I can be there by two-thirty."

Without waiting for a reply, he turned, walked silently across the highly-polished floor, and let himself out the door.

"Someone should lock the damned thing before some other varmint walks through it." Faith wrapped a protective arm around her sister's shoulder.

Hope shook her head. "Eddie's defection is ancient history, girls. And it has no relevance to the here and now. I had no idea that Daddy was doing business with him, though." She glanced at Margaret and the other church ladies who were peeking around the kitchen door. "We're going to say goodbye and let you get home. Thank you again for everything you did today. We truly appreciate it."

"You going to be all right, honey?" Margaret Ann asked Hope.

"Somehow, everything will be fine, but a few extra prayers won't hurt anything," Hope said with a wink.

Back in the limousine, the women sat in silence as the driver wound his way back through town to return them to the Blessing Farm.

Faith stared out the window. "I've been so wrapped up raising my two boys; it's been two hard years since I visited."

"And I was always thinking there would be more time," said Grace without looking at the others. "One assignment seemed to follow right after another. They all seemed so important . . . ."

Hope patted her sisters' hands. "Remember Daddy always said, 'God has made everything appropriate to its time.' He missed you, but he was proud that you both made your way in life."

Hope hummed softly as she set the dining room table for breakfast. Grace was at the stove scrambling eggs while Faith manned the toaster. *Just like old times.*

"Come and get it," Grace said, pushing through the doorway with a platter heaped high with eggs and bacon. Her sisters filtered to the table and sat down at their places.

Faith ran her slender finger along the wide mahogany chair seat. "I've tried several times to do this type of embroidery, but it never comes out as well as Mom's." The threads in the ruby roses and the persimmon poppies were almost as vibrant as when they were first sewn.

Hope laughed. "Remember Daddy's face the day he came in to eat and found all the chairs apart because Mom got so wrapped up in the new seat covers she completely forgot about dinner?"

"Oh yeah, I can still see his expression. If I remember right, he and Grace made us grilled cheese sandwiches and tomato soup," Faith said.

Grace frowned. "I don't remember that. Are you sure I'm the one who helped Father with dinner?"

Faith giggled. "Yes, you did. You were very proud of your plate of 'triangles', as you put it."

Hope pointed to a side chair in the corner. "That one hasn't held up as well as the others. Someone or something must have snagged it and pulled some thread through it."

"Bet I can stitch that up, later." Faith said. "It'll give me something to do this evening."

Grace passed the platter of eggs to Faith. "Food's getting cold."

"Hope, say the blessing?" Faith folded her hands over her plate.

"Woops," said Grace, with a slice of toast half way to her mouth.

Hope closed her eyes and folded her hands. "Lord, thank you for blessing us with this food and each other."

"Amen," her sisters said in unison.

"Can we eat now?" Grace grumbled.

"Dig in," Hope said. "What are *your* twins up to these days, Faith?"

Faith placed her fork on her plate. "Well, what do you mean? Their height or their teenage antics?" She took a sip of coffee and grimaced. "Man, that's hot. Anyway, they're spending a few weeks with their father, the wonderful Mr. Beauregard Walker, at his family ranch outside Fort Worth. The boys were excited about participating in a local rodeo. I only hope they don't break their necks, or I'll break his."

Grace nodded. "I'll help you get rid of the body."

That's the twins I remember. Hope laughed. "Rodeo sounds exciting."

"Yes, Beau is all about the exciting part of life, at least until he's bored with it," Faith said. "But the boys find him much more fun than me since he acts more like their age than his own."

"Grace, how was Army life in Israel?" Hope asked. "Daddy always talked about doing a springtime pilgrimage to the Holy Land. As engineers, do you get time to explore much beyond the base?"

"I did get to see some of Jerusalem before heading out into the desert for months on end." She wiped her mouth with her napkin. "I remember how Father talked about us going there on a pilgrimage someday. People from all around the world and all religions are there."

"What was it like for you?" Hope asked again.

Grace put down her fork and looked at Hope. "I found it to be a country of contradictions. You'd think that Israel would be the most peaceful place on earth. After all, the Dome of the Rock was built at Jerusalem as a symbol of the unity of the Jewish, Christian, and Islamic religions. Instead, it's a land of constant conflict and destruction, co-existing with exquisite natural beauty."

"Did you go to the Wailing Wall?" asked Faith.

"I went with some of my team after we were told it was not to be missed. We were only in Israel maybe a week at that time. It was a moving experience. Even for a person who has taken a turn away from religion."

Like you, my precious sister? "I'll bet it's really beautiful." Hope tossed her napkin to the side and then rested her elbows on the table.

Grace stood and pushed in her chair. "It is, in a haunting and ancient sort of way. Powerful is a better word, I think. It's very spiritual, regardless of one's individual beliefs or lack of them."

She collected her plate, mug, and utensils and headed for the kitchen. "I think I'll go set up Daddy's office for the reading of the will."

Hope smiled at her sister. "You go ahead and I'll take care of cleaning up breakfast. Could you go through the mail I stuffed in the top drawer and make sure there's nothing important in it?"

Grace opened the pocket doors to the office. She raised the shades to let in the sunlight and ran her hand across the old scarred wooden desk where she and her sisters had carved their names at their father's request. The week after their mother had died, Percy had insisted on it so he could keep his girls with him all the time. She'd forgotten about that.

Settling into her father's chair, Grace squared her shoulders. She slid open the middle drawer and pulled out the packet of envelopes Hope had hastily stuffed inside, and reached for the silver rose-patterned letter opener.

She smiled. *Hello, Mama.* The three girls had saved their allowance for six months to buy their mother a special Christmas gift that would last forever. How her mother had admired it in the Treasures antique shop window. *Is Treasures still open in Merciful these days?* She'd have to find out before she returned to duty.

In a few minutes, all the mail had been opened and filed in the wastebasket, except the last letter. The return address of a legal firm in the upper left-hand corner looked ominous. Grace held her breath as she opened it and pulled out the documents.

"Oh, no. This can't be true." She strode to the door. "Hope, Faith, get in here on the double!"

They appeared in the doorway. Faith had the carpet sweeper in her hand.

"What's going on?" Hope asked.

"This." She shoved the papers into Hope's hand. "How long have you known about this?"

Hope scanned the legal document with its official heading. "My lord, I know that Dad was struggling with some loans at Betty Jo's bank, but I never dreamed he was facing foreclosure!" She shook her head and passed the papers to Faith. "That must be what Betty Jo meant when she said he didn't own the place anymore. That's why Betty Jo was looking for the mortgage note. They can't foreclose without that."

"Foreclosure?" Faith screeched. "Does Betty Jo own *every* asset of the Blessing family? Foreclosure. I can't believe this." She glared at Hope. "How could you know he was in so much trouble and not tell us?"

"Hey, I remortgaged my building to loan Daddy money to prevent this. I thought he was going to be okay," Hope said, turning pale. "And he would have been if he'd had more time, I know it." She clutched her hands together. "This probably means J B Clark Savings and Loan will be looking for my house next. Dad was supposed to give me back the money to pay the balloon note."

Grace snatched the foreclosure notice from Faith's hands. *I can't believe Hope fell for that. How could my perfect sister have messed up like this?* "Maybe there's some life insurance. Or, maybe it's just time to give it all to her and minimize your losses. Move to Texas, be closer to Faith. You can cut hair anywhere. At least you'd be away from that bitch."

Hope squared her shoulders and wagged her finger at her sister. "You don't even own a home, so you have no idea what it means to lose one, let alone everything that generations have worked for. I have no intention of giving up without a fight."

"Do you have the money to pay her? How the hell do you fight back without money?" Faith asked.

"No, I don't have the money, but I can pray for a solution. There's got to be a way I haven't thought of. Maybe we can sell the paid-off trucks for enough to pay the arrears," Hope said. "At least keep the homestead. We don't need the trucking company, I guess." She sat down in one of the parlor chairs and put her head in her hands.

Grace patted Hope's shoulder, and placed the papers back on the desk. *You always were the optimist, Sis.* "Sorry I snapped at you, but I still wish you'd have let us know what's been going on here."

"To be honest, I always thought we'd be able to handle it.

And it's not like I was keeping close tabs on Daddy. He wasn't senile or anything close to it." She looked at them and sighed. "Besides, you've both had your own lives to take care of. You deserve your own lives."

"Doesn't God want you to have a life too, Hope?" Grace asked.

Without looking up, Hope nodded. The silence in the room was stifling.

"Well, let's finish cleaning up in here," Faith said, clearing her throat. She ran the carpet sweeper across the threadbare Oriental rug. "It's getting late."

Hope raised her head and looked through tears at her sister. "Mr. Highspring will be barging his way in soon. I wonder what he knows about this foreclosure business . . . ."

Chapter Four

Resurrection

The chime rang twice in the Grandfather clock just as Highspring knocked on the front door of the farmhouse.

Faith swung open the heavy oak door, resisting the urge to slam it on his Florsheim™ shoes. Instead she invited him inside. "Grace and Hope will meet us in the office in a minute. I guess you know where to go, right?"

"Sure, I know my way around."

I'll bet you do.

"How've you been, Faith?" Eddie stepped inside and closed the door.

Oh, life's just hunky dory. "Life has its ups and downs, but my boys and I do all right."

Eddie nodded. "Your father sure loved hearing about the twins and their escapades. He'd always tell me stories and smile. He sure was proud of you."

Too bad we didn't know it. She led the way into the office and took a seat on one of the tall overstuffed armchairs. In front of the brick fireplace was a brass hearth screen in the shape of a truck cab, a project from Faith's days in welding school. Two-inch wooden blinds were pulled tight against the summer heat.

Grace and Hope appeared in the doorway. Hope carried a large glass pitcher of sweet tea and Grace held four ice-packed glasses. They proceeded to fill them, and Grace handed the first one to Eddie.

"Thank you, ladies," said Eddie as he fiddled with his laptop computer. Hope's gaze fixed on the back pockets of his khaki's as he leaned over the computer.

Sis, I swear you are checking out his backside. Faith nudged Hope with her elbow. "Not too shabby," she whispered.

Hope's face turned the color of a poppy. She turned and dropped onto the sofa and clasped her hands in her lap. Grace sat beside her, chuckling.

"Enough, both of you," hissed Hope. "There is nothing funny about this at all."

Eddie turned to face the three women. "Your father redid his will about six months ago, though his health was fine. That's when he came to see me. He wanted to tell you his wishes himself, so he worked with my office and made a video will. You'll each get a copy of the disk, but for today, we'll view mine."

He hit a key on his laptop and a light blue screen appeared. A second later, Percival Blessing was in the middle of the computer screen. His lanky six-feet, four-inch frame seemed less daunting than they remembered, his tanned face and silvered hair thinner than it had been a year ago.

He wore his Sunday suit—the blue pin-striped one he'd been buried in yesterday.

"Hello girls," Percy began, "it's nice to see you all together again."

Hope didn't think the pain in her heart could get any worse. Before her eyes stood her father, right in the very same room where she and her sisters now sat. *Oh Daddy, what I wouldn't give to touch your face one more time.* She swiped away a tear.

"It's been a long time since you girls have been together in this house. And I'm sorry. I know it's my fault," Percy said to his daughters as the DVD played on.

Faith looked at Hope. "What's he talking about? We grew up; we left home, built lives. Isn't that what we were supposed to do?"

"Exactly the normal thing to do," said Grace.

Hope nodded. Or at least that's how I thought it should work.

"Take a breath, ladies," said Eddie, "this isn't going to be easy."

Percy glanced down. He unfolded and folded his hands before looking back at the camera. "Your mother, Sarah, was the brains of this operation. She kept my books in perfect order. Yes sirree, your mama kept the household and the trucking company running like a finely tuned diesel. Praise the Lord, me and Sarah are together again." He paused and pulled his trademark white cotton handkerchief from his back pocket and wiped his eyes.

The sisters sat without speaking. Hope let the tears run down her face unheeded; Grace swallowed hard and cleared her throat, while Faith dabbed at her eyes with a tissue.

"I love you all so much that it hurts. Hope, I owe you a long overdue apology. Lord knows I should have let you go on with your life after your mother passed, but I couldn't do it. I needed you so much. We all did. I had no idea how to go on, let alone help Faith and Grace grow up to be the women their mother would have raised them to be."

Hope gasped. *Oh Papa, you don't owe me anything.* Faith patted her hand.

Their father continued. "Faith and Grace, you two may have been unexpected, but never think that you were not miracles to your mother and me. I've always treasured you and have been proud of the women you've become."

Eddie paused the recording. "Need a break? Something to drink, maybe?" he asked.

Grace nodded. "I could use a brandy. How about you girls?" she asked, getting to her feet and walking to the liquor cabinet hidden in the bookcase.

"Count me in," Faith said. "Hope?"

"Sure," Hope murmured. "Eddie?"

He looked at Hope for a moment, and then shook his head. "Take a rain check, but thanks."

With snifters in hand, the three women returned to their seats, and faced the screen on Eddie's computer. He hit the play button and Percy was once again speaking to his daughters.

"Things are a mess here. Though it's not all my fault, some of it is. Your mother had the business sense. I loved her and the road and didn't worry about the rest. I probably should have learned more about the practical stuff, but I never realized how fast life could change."

He took a drink of water and looked back at them. "Hope, I'm sorry about that loan, honey. I was sure I could get the company profitable again before that balloon payment came due. But," he hesitated and looked away from the camera for a moment, "things started to happen. I lost customers that were with me for years. I lost drivers on the spot. Guys I had trusted and could count on, just up and left me without warning. You girls are going to have to work together to get Hope out of trouble that she wouldn't have if it weren't for me."

"Hope?" asked Grace.

"Shhh," she replied.

"Here's the assignment, girls. You all work together and you just might be able to keep the homestead and the trucks out of the clutches of Betty Jo Clark. If you don't, everything is gone, including Hope's home and the beauty shop."

"Oh damn," Faith whispered."I can't do this now."

Percy nodded at them from the computer screen. "You all

know that when your great-grandparents settled this land, they founded Merciful. But Betty Jo will destroy this town. She's a very hurtful woman. I can't explain why, but it just seems to be the way of it."

He cleared his throat and continued. "Grace and Faith, time you came home. There's plenty of room here for you both, and Faith, your boys too, if you want. You all figure out why I lost the Southern Gypsum and the railroad contracts, get 'em back and you'll be able to pay off those loans in six months. There's an insurance policy, and Eddie is the trustee. If you don't get things worked out, Eddie gets paid from the life insurance proceeds. Then he'll split what's left over with you three, but seventy-five thousand isn't going all that far."

"Oh damn," echoed Eddie.

"That's it, girls." Percy smiled his trademark smile." If I hadn't seen that old Matlock rerun, I'd never have thought of this will thing, but I'm glad I did. Gave me a chance to say all the things that I should have said years ago. Oh, and Eddie has a personal recording from me to each of you. I hope they help you. Remember that me and your mother love you, no matter what. May the Lord bless you on this journey."

The computer screen went dark and the room was silent. Eddie powered off his computer and rested his hip against the edge of Percy's desk.

"Eddie, if our father had no idea he was going to die, how did he know he wouldn't have gotten the company out of trouble? This video seems to be pretty timely for a healthy man," Grace said.

"He was in his seventies and struggling with some big financial headaches. Maybe the stress he was under forced him to do the will. I promised him that he could update it as often as he wanted."

"Well, struggling seems to be an understatement. We found foreclosure paperwork in Dad's desk." Hope pointed at him. "How the hell do we get out of that, Eddie?"

He rubbed his chin with the fingers of his left hand. "That's not a good thing. I wish he'd told me about that." He stood and paced behind the desk. "Depending on when he was served, I can file an injunction and put everything into a Chapter 11 reorganizational bankruptcy. Betty Jo can't touch you once I've done that. Once we get the plan approved in Tallahassee, you'll have time to get the company up and running, pay the creditors."

"Will Betty Jo have to approve the settlement?"

He nodded. "She will, but you'll still have thirty to sixty days before that happens, probably closer to sixty. She can't even call you about it once we've filed, though. The courts are backed up with people going under these days. They'll encourage her bank to negotiate new terms."

Gee, good luck with that. Hope sighed.

Faith looked at Hope, then addressed Eddie. "Can you save Hope's place, too?"

"If Hope wants to file a Chapter 13 bankruptcy, we can buy enough time to save her, too. Or at least give it a real good try. But her property isn't part of your father's estate, so they'd be two different legal actions."

"How much will that cost?" Hope asked.

"A few thousand, mostly in filing and court fees. We can work all that out later."

Grace shook her head. "Do we know how bad the financial picture is?"

"I don't," said Hope. "He had a bookkeeper that I met once or twice. If we have to, I can call her to help us go over things and pay her for her time. But about a year ago, Daddy's drivers started to leave. Two of the four long-timers are still with him, though. He started driving again to pick up the slack. He felt responsible for the ones that stayed and when he got behind on the truck payments, he tried to sell the newest rig to get out from under. In this economy with fuel prices so high, there are more trucks for sale than Detroit has empty factories. I took a loan at the bank with really lousy terms, but I was sure Daddy would get things up and running again."

Faith frowned. "When Dad lost the contracts, nobody told him why?"

"Someone underbid him, I think. He was on time and never had a shortage or any safety violations and he was sure he'd be okay. He still had several other steady customers, but longer hauls were less profitable for him."

"Does he still have the Conagra work?" Faith asked.

"I think so," Hope said.

Eddie cleared his throat. "May I make a suggestion, ladies?"

"Could we stop you?" asked Grace.

"Since it appears we'll be joined at the hip until we get this resolved, guess you might as well," said Hope, raising her chin as she spoke to him. Daddy, what have you done?

He ignored their jabs. "The way I see it, the first decision is whether or not you three can agree to live and work together."

Grace narrowed her eyes. "I don't see why we have to move back home to make this work. I'll just sign my portion over to Hope. I have some money saved up. If she needs it she can have it."

"Percy made me his executor. He emphasized that you either all work together, or you all walk away. It's an all or nothing proposition."

Faith's eyes filled with tears. "I'm sorry Hope, but I can't just move back here. Isiah and Joshua still have a year of high school to finish. I can't tear them away from Bufford right now."

"And I haven't decided if I'm retiring this year or not, but even if I do, I had no intention of coming back here to stay. I love New Mexico." Grace got to her feet.

Hope stared out the window at the tall garage bays that represented the Amazing Grace Trucking Company. Their past and maybe their future. Her sisters didn't understand.

"Mom and Daddy gave us all they could. They gave each

other all they could. This homestead may not be much, but it is ours and I just hate the idea that Betty Jo will get it, for a fraction of what it's worth, and turn around and sell it to some Yankee investor to build McMansions on. That idea just makes me sick."

"Happens every day," Grace said. "We have no idea how much work or time this will take even if we all agree to give it a try. And I'm not sure I'm even willing to."

"I know, but I don't care. I won't agree to let this go quietly," said Hope.

"A compromise, perhaps?" interrupted Eddie.

"What?" the three women snapped in unison.

He moved behind the desk and dropped into Percy's old tall-backed leather chair. "Give it thirty days. Sixty, tops. Faith, can your boys spend the whole summer with Beau if necessary?"

"I don't know how his new wife would feel about that, but if I could make it worth his while, they might be more agreeable. I can't move out of state without going back to court and getting permission to relocate, and that would take money I don't have."

Eddie stood. "I can petition the Court for you to move to Florida if it comes to that. You could sell or rent your home in Texas and the boys could finish school in the same high school that you attended, here. How about you let Beau off the hook for child support this summer and maybe he'd be happier about keeping the boys longer. What do you think?"

"Okay, Mr. Highhorse-Highspring, if you can get him to go for the child support deal for the rest of the summer, I'll commit to giving this a couple months," Faith said, tapping her index finger on the edge of the desk.

He walked around the desk toward Grace. "You probably have time accumulated. Can you take a leave of absence, or vacation, or something?"

Grace thought a minute. "I guess I could, but this isn't

going to be fixed in thirty days."

"Not entirely," he said, "but we'll know in thirty days if the plan will work. In sixty days we'll know if you can pull it off."

Hope smiled. "Well, if we don't incur any new expenses and we can keep at least three of the four trucks on the road, we have a chance, girls."

"I thought you said Daddy only had two steady drivers left," Faith said.

Hope looked at Grace and lifted her left brow. "Grace has her commercial driver's license. She can drive one of the trucks."

"Oh, sure. Just what I want to do," Grace grumbled. "Back to working like a grunt."

"Well, the only commercial license I have is to do hair and that's about as far from a truck as a person can get. The only thing I can bring is my business knowledge. I can scout up work, keep the books, that kind of stuff."

"What about the beauty salon?" asked Faith.

"I can either run it part time or see if the girls who work with me want to take it over for the summer. I can help them with supplies and the books there, too. If they get backed up, I'll fill in when I can."

"So, Percy's girls, will you give it thirty days?" Eddie asked.

The sisters looked at each other in silence.

Grace spoke for the trio. "Count us in—at least for thirty days. We'll talk again about the sixty."

After her sisters had gone to the kitchen to start dinner, Hope sat on the back porch. *Daddy, can we really make this work?*

An owl hooted and a bob-white whistled in reply and she laughed. She sat with a glass of bourbon in hand and listened to the frogs sing by the creek. The smell of fresh-mown hay hung in the air.

She'd worked hard to give her sisters the chance to break free of Merciful's small-town hold. She'd wanted them to have the choice to go or stay, something she'd never had. She was crushed that they couldn't wait to leave when they'd graduated high school, but at some level she'd understood. Hadn't she been ready to fly far and wide before her mother's death? Would she have returned if she'd gotten the chance to go to college and marry Eddie?

When her husband died in Betty Jo's bed four years ago, Hope should have left the town and humiliation behind as soon as his sorry butt was buried, but once again, she couldn't leave her father behind. So she'd stayed.

Now that she could leave, was she strong enough to stay? Did she have enough fight left to carry on yet another battle for this patch of dirt and some run-down trucks? *So what, my ancestors founded the town. Who really cares?*

She finished her drink, sighed, and got to her feet. If the good Lord wanted her to win this, she'd have everything she needed. And if she was taking on Betty Jo out of foolish pride, then she didn't have a prayer.

Chapter Five

Roads to Home

Grace flipped the burgers on the grill, and inhaled the warm Florida air. *Lord, I'd forgotten how lovely humidity could be.* The hot, dry, Israeli desert home, where she'd spent the last eighteen months, didn't compare to Florida's warm and wet climate.

Faith moved the bowls of food around on the table to make room for the pitcher of tea. Everyone took their seats at the glass-topped table.

"It's really pleasant out here tonight. The air seems to be cooling." Faith undid the clip that held her hair up off her shoulders. "Austin is drier than it is here."

"Those ceiling fans help keep that breeze moving." Hope pointed upward. "But, nothing we can do about the humidity, I'm afraid."

Faith shrugged. "Nothing we can do about a lot of things. Let's dig in, girls."

"Wait. Hold up a minute," Hope said. "Let's give thanks first." She held out both hands. Around the table, they formed a chain.

"Lord, we learned some unpleasant news today. We could hear worse tomorrow. But whatever lies ahead, give us the strength to conquer it together."

"Amen," they said in unison.

Grace looked at her sister. "Living together here is going to take some getting used to, whatever arrangements we make. Hopefully, we can get the trucking company to make money and clean up Father's finances. How did you make out with Beau and the boys, Faith?"

"Beau has agreed to keep them for the summer. I don't know how his new wife feels about that, but he's just delighted not to have to send me that support check every month. If I have to stay longer, we'll have to talk again. I want them with me, not him."

Grace nodded. She didn't want to stay here. But then, in her years in the Army, she'd had to go places she didn't want to go, too. This was just another job that needed doing, but would she be here to get it done?

She picked up her iced tea and held it in the air as a salute. "Well, ladies, here's to successful resurrections. And while you're praying for things, better pray that I get that leave of absence approved or you can count me out."

Monday morning, the sun shone through the windows in the study where Hope sat on the floor amidst piles of paper and folders. Faith and Grace had gotten an early start and gone to the garages to begin an inventory of the equipment and supplies on hand.

A knock on the door startled Hope. She got up off her knees, wiped her hands on her jeans, and went to answer it. *Bet I know who that is. Bitch.*

As expected, Betty Jo was on the other side. "Good morning, Hope," she said, pushing past her like she already owned the place.

"Well, it *is* morning," Hope replied. "I expected you earlier, actually."

Betty Jo smoothed her white linen skirt, and then adjusted the matching jacket. The Tommy Bahama™ look went well with her black and white Spectator™ pumps. "I have a business to run, and Monday mornings are always very busy at the bank."

"I imagine that's so. We're busy here, too. The study isn't fit for company, so let's talk in the dining room." Hope led the way.

Betty Jo sat down and crossed her legs, leaning back in the chair like a panther who had just eaten a large meal. "You know why I'm here. I had your father served with foreclosure paperwork two weeks ago. And, your note on the shop is due in another thirty days. If you don't pay that note in full, I'll be pursuing legal action against you as well."

Hope looked Betty Jo in the eye. "We found the paperwork so we're aware of your intentions." She leaned forward on the table. "Did you find what you were looking for the other night?"

"Never mind about the other night. I had every right to be here."

Like hell. "I disagree. This is our home, not your collateral and you have no right to be here without an invitation."

Betty Jo's red-polished talons waved her dismissal of the Hope's comment. "Only a matter of days. You should really be packing, you know."

Hope clenched her fists and raised her chin. "Our attorney has informed us that he'll be filing to protect us from all debt-related legal actions starting today."

"Oh, and who would your attorney be?"

"Someone you know quite well. Eddie Highspring. I'm sure if you try real hard, you'll remember your ex-husband." *Although what he ever saw in you is way beyond me.*

The flush on Betty Jo's face was redder than an English tea rose. "Well, if I were you, I'd be hoping he's a better lawyer than he was a husband."

"I'm sure he's learned his lesson when it comes to dealing with you," Hope said, getting to her feet. "It's time for you to leave. Under the circumstances I'm not even sure you should be here at all."

Betty Jo stood and faced off with Hope, ignoring her comment. "I always get what I want, remember that."

The porch door slammed and seconds later, Faith and Grace stood in the doorway. Grace stepped forward. "Didn't Daddy always tell us to keep the doors closed so that the varmints stayed out?"

Betty Jo glared at the twins. "I'll be seeing you all again soon, I'm sure." She turned on her heel and let herself out the front door.

"So," started Faith, "how'd she take the news that we were going to fight her?"

Hope shrugged. "About like you'd think. She intends to take it all and won't be satisfied until she does."

Faith put her arm around Hope's shoulder. "That woman won't be satisfied until she's dead. She's got a hole inside her that all of Daddy's trucks couldn't fill."

"I don't think I'll rest easy until she's in her grave. But for now, we've got a lot of work to do," Hope said.

Grace stood with her hands on her hips, her feet slightly apart, lips pursed. "Faith and I have to leave tomorrow to take care of some things so we can stay on with you. We've got the drivers coming to meet with us at the shop later this afternoon. Maybe you can throw together some lunch, and we'll meet on the porch in an hour."

Hope stood in the kitchen and stared through the window. What if these guys want more than we can pay? What if they're tired of working for a broke-down, two-bit company? Will they even work for three women?

She stood in the quiet and took a deep breath. *Lord, I'm sorry to be doubting your plan. You know what we need, so I'll stop frettin'. Help us to serve you. Amen.*

Showtime, thought Grace. She glanced at her sisters.

The threesome watched through the large plate glass window in the office loft in the garage. The Cheech and Chong look-a-likes got out of a black pickup truck and walked side by side up the wide concrete driveway. When they'd disappeared into the garage, the girls moved away from the window.

"Come on in," called Grace from her father's tattered leather chair.

The drivers entered the small room and introduced themselves. Faith and Hope stood beside the steel desk on either side of Grace.

"We wanted to bring you guys up to speed on the future of the company," Grace said. "We need some information from you before we proceed, though."

Manny shifted his feet. "What do you need to know?"

"Do you know why the other drivers walked off the job?" Faith asked.

"New outfit in the area made big promises. More money, fewer miles," Patrick said, stuffing his hands into his front pants pockets.

"Why didn't you two go?" Grace asked.

Patrick smiled. "Your father was a good man, and he was true to his word." He pushed his hands deeper into his pockets and looked away from them. "When my wife Colleen had surgery, your dad helped with the medical bills."

"And when my kid got hurt playing football," Manny said, "and I had to stay home with him, your father paid me and let me keep my job. He didn't have to do that. You don't walk away from people like Percy Blessing."

The air in the room seemed to close in on Grace as she realized maybe she didn't really know her father after all. But he'd left them in a real mess and that was where they had to focus. She leaned forward and tented her fingers under her chin. "What about the contracts? Was it the same outfit that outbid him on those?"

"Yeah," the two men answered in unison.

"What's the name?" she asked.

"Mattheson Transport Company, over near Lake City," Patrick answered.

Grace jotted notes on the pad in front of her. "Okay, here's our plan of action. We'd like to know if we can count on you to stay on, at least for a while."

"Let's hear what you have," Manny said.

Faith moved to the front of the desk, closer to the drivers. "We're thinking that if we can keep three trucks on the road, win a couple of new contracts, even if they're longer distances, we can generate enough income to keep your wages paid and pay the bills."

The drivers had to see their solidarity. Grace stood and joined Faith. "Look," Grace started, "all the vendors are willing to keep working with us because our father kept them paid within thirty days. We've got a good location here, only a few miles from the Interstate. We have no environmental issues, no neighbors that don't like our trucks rumbling along Magnolia. The rigs are in decent condition. But the bank is out for blood. If we slip up, they'll get everything."

Hope looked at the men. "Are you in? Will you help us keep Amazing Grace on the highways?"

Patrick and Manny glanced at each other. "If you can keep us working and promise us our regular pay for the work done, we'll stay on with you all."

Grace stood and held out her hand. "Welcome aboard, gentlemen, to the next generation of Amazing Grace Trucking Company."

Through the dusty wooden blinds on the window, Grace watched Hope and Faith walk back to the house. She sat in her father's chair and absorbed the quiet. *Maybe we have a chance to succeed after all.*

Confident that they'd leave her alone in the garage until

diner time, she took the CD from the top drawer and held it in her hands. The label read, "To Grace."

She'd tossed and turned last night wondering what her father had wanted to say to her that was so difficult that he had to record it. And of course, she wasn't sure she wanted to know at all.

She opened the disk drive on the laptop, slipped in the CD, and pushed the drive closed. As the computer drive began to whir, she stabbed the stop button and jumped out of the chair. Dust swirled in the air at the sudden motion.

She charged to the front window and wiped her sweaty palms on her denim-clad thighs. Her chest felt like she'd swallowed a boulder. Damn it, anyway.

Squaring her shoulders, she marched back to the desk and glared at the computer screen. *I'm a big girl. Whatever it is, I can handle it.*

Grace shoved the chair out of the way and reached for the mouse to click the "play" button.

A box appeared on the screen. "Open file?"

Grace stared at the question as though she'd been asked to explain the Theory of Relativity. *Well, yes or no? She felt like she was going to throw up.*

She took a deep breath and clicked on "yes." Her father's face filled the screen.

"My dear, Grace. This is my letter to you. I know I haven't told you how proud I am of the woman you are. And of the things you do for people all around the world."

She punched the pause button. "Would it have killed you to say that when you were alive?" she shouted at her father's image frozen on the screen. "Never once, not one time did you tell me you were proud of me." Her throat clogged with unshed tears as she dropped into the chair. For several minutes she concentrated on breathing slowly until she'd fought off the sorrow that threatened to break her down. She hit the button to resume playing the recording.

"One thing I need you to do is mend fences with Hope. It's okay that you're angry with me, but she doesn't deserve it."

"Oh, stop." Grace jabbed the stop button, ejected the CD, and stuffed it back in the case.

Dammit. Just like always. It's all about Hope. Why am I surprised?

With a sigh, she clicked off the light and slammed the office door behind her. She had packing to do. She couldn't afford to miss that flight to New Mexico.

Maybe I won't come back.

Chapter Six

Wrath

"Hey, Faith," called Grace from the foot of the tall, aluminum ladder. "You missed a spot!" Dressed in fatigue pants covered with pockets of all sizes and uses and a moss green tee-shirt, her bare feet mocked the otherwise military look.

Faith, in cutoff jeans and a sleeveless button-down shirt, retaliated by heaving a huge, sopping, soapy sponge at her sister. "You get up here and do this, then," she said. "My shoulder's killing me with all this scrubbing anyway." She straightened on the ladder and pulled her hair from the band that held it back. In three twists, she had it tied up again.

Hope smiled and watched her sisters' antics. It felt right to have them home, even if most everything else felt wrong. She'd spent all day Tuesday calling Percy's old clients and fielding calls from his creditors. Thankfully, no creditors were seriously behind yet, but even with a business bond still in place, they were nervous about extending credit now that word had 'leaked' out about the foreclosure.

Leaked. Yeah, right. Betty Jo had made sure everyone in

the state of Florida knew they'd defaulted on their loans.

So, on Wednesday morning, the Blessing sisters splashed buckets of soapy water on the rigs at dawn's first light. They scrubbed the dust and debris from metal and tires. Grace's power hose rinsed the soapy solution as the trucks gleamed in the early morning sun.

Hope helped by drying all the surfaces she could reach. She climbed around the cab on the frame and the fenders much as she had on Saturday mornings when she was a child. Her father had paid her five dollars for each truck wash back then.

A white Ford Focus drove up the driveway. Reverend Shawn Jackson unfolded his long frame and climbed out of the car. He limped over to them and tipped his wide-brimmed straw hat.

"Mornin', ladies. I just stopped by to see how y'all are doing."

Hope dropped her towel beside the bucket at her feet and wiped her hands on her jeans. "Welcome, Shawn." Hope embraced her father's long-time friend.

Grace and Faith trotted over to join them. "Why are you limping?" Grace asked.

"Oh, I tripped at the cemetery and went down on my bad knee. Just a little clumsy, I guess."

Faith nodded. "I didn't notice you limping at the church. I'm sorry you were injured."

"It's nothing a little time won't heal. Thank you," the minister said.

Hope motioned toward the house. "Why don't we go sit on the porch and get something cool to drink?"

Shawn Jackson settled in the chair at the head of the table and Hope sat beside him. Faith and Grace went to the kitchen for drinks.

"Looks like you girls are getting into the trucking business."

Hope nodded. "That's our goal. Put it back in the black." She told Reverend Jackson the details of her father's will. "So, for the next month we're working together to get the business back on solid ground."

"I see some improvements here already." Reverend Jackson winced with pain as he moved in his seat.

"Are you okay?" Hope asked. "Can I get you something?"

"Got anything for pain? The knee is still a bit swollen and when I move a certain way it hurts."

Hope went into the kitchen for some aspirin and a glass of water. Her sisters were almost done making a pitcher of fresh lemonade.

"Here you go," Hope said, handing the pills to the reverend.

"Thank you," he said. "Eddie told me you girls were going to have a tough time reviving the business. Your daddy confided his troubles to me, too. I'm here to see how I can help you."

Hope leaned on the table. "Do you know anything about Mattheson Transport Company?"

Reverend Jackson tugged on his ponytail, deep in thought. "Mattheson . . . Mattheson . . . that name rings a bell but I can't . . . ." His blue eyes widened. "Mattheson. I remember Betty Jo was married to a Craig Mattheson at one time."

"Why, that sleazy witch." Hope banged the table so hard the glass of water splashed. "I should have known she had a hand in this."

"Whoa, missy." The Reverend waved his hands. "Calm down. It could be a coincidence. I don't know if Betty Jo has any connection to this or not."

"I'm sure she's behind this whole takeover mess." Hope clenched her fists and bit her upper lip. "She wants to ruin me, my family, and the family business. She hates me, and I hate her."

Faith and Grace came through the doorway with the lemonade and some tall glasses. Her sisters stopped in their tracks. "What's going on?" they asked in unison.

Shawn Jackson patted Hope's hand. "Your sister suspects that Betty Jo is behind all the troubles your father's had. But even if that's true, you have to cast these feelings aside. All that hate will make you sick. I know it's hard, but you've got to do it."

Tears trickled down Hope's face. "This goes back a long way with Betty Jo and me. Eddie and I were in love in high school but she always wanted him. She did everything she could to break us up, including getting him drunk, seducing him, and getting pregnant from their one-night stand. And of course, you know all about my husband's affair with her. Now she's gone and killed my father with all this damned stress."

The Reverend handed her his handkerchief. "Hope, I know you're hurt. I know how hard it is to forgive people who keep hurting us, but we've got to do it. We've all done things we're not proud of. Everyone one of us is human, not divine." He looked down as his voice lowered. "Therefore, we're all flawed in one way or another."

"Maybe," Hope said. "But I never did anything to hurt Betty Jo or anybody else that I know of. Not on purpose anyway."

Reverend pointed at Faith and Grace. "How about the years you and your sisters have been estranged?"

"That wasn't my fault. I don't think they've stayed away just because of me," Hope said. But the nagging sadness in her heart made her statement a lie. "I always gave them all I could and put them first. If that was wrong, then we'll just chalk it up to being an eighteen year-old 'parent.'"

"We have to let things go from the past and move forward. That's what the Lord wants us to do." Shawn nodded. "That's what your daddy would want. Remember, I'll be praying for you, but let me know if there's anything else I can do for you."

He glanced at his watch. "I've got to go. I have a lot of work at the church." He held on to the table for balance and stood.

"Thanks for stopping by, Reverend. We appreciate the support," Grace said. She and Faith remained seated, their lemonade untouched.

"I'll walk you out," Hope said.

They made their way slowly to his car. He slid into the

driver's seat and turned the key. "Have Eddie check out Mattheson Transport Company."

"I will certainly do that." Hope nodded. "Take care of that knee."

The good reverend waved and backed out of the driveway.

When Hope got back to the porch, her sisters were gone. She poured a glass of lemonade and dropped into the rattan loveseat. "This set really needs some new cushions," she muttered to the air.

She rested her head back and closed her eyes. Sure, she was angry as hell over Matthew's infidelity. And it hurt even more that he was unfaithful with Betty Jo of all people, but was she really still bitter about things that happened when they were teenagers? Until she'd seen Eddie again on Saturday, she'd thought she was over all that high school stuff, but maybe not. The reverend was right. Her father would not be pleased with her if that was the case.

And what about her sisters? Did they hate her for doing the best she could to fill in for their mother? Had she done it for them, her father, or herself? Maybe the only important thing was making it right with them now . . . .

"Sweet Home Alabama" blared across the yard from the garages. She could hear Faith singing in her slightly off-key way, while Grace yelled at her to shut up. Hope got to her feet. It was obviously time to face the past.

She hiked out to the shop and pushed the creaky door open. Grace and Faith looked in her direction, then resumed what they were doing.

"Do you need any help out here?" Hope asked.

Grace shrugged but didn't reply.

Faith answered with a smile. "Sure, we're just doing inventory on the parts and tools out here. Grab a sheet of paper and a box of stuff, and write down what you find."

"And how would I know what to write down?" Hope asked.

"I wouldn't know a wrench from a tire iron."

Grace snickered. "No, Miss Prim, you wouldn't. Daddy's favorite daughter never spent a lick of time out here, did she?"

Faith gasped. "Grace, you promised."

"Promised what?" Hope interrupted. "You twins always had secrets between you, but it's time to grow up."

"No secret," Grace said. "Faith doesn't want to talk about the past. She doesn't want to upset you."

"Maybe it's time you two were honest with me about what's been bothering you all these years."

"Oh sure. We'll just have a sisterly heart to heart and fix it all, right?" Grace tossed her pen and pad on the old steel desk.

Hope sighed. "If we don't talk about it, will it go away or be the same?"

"What's it matter? In thirty days we can all go back to our regularly-scheduled lives, right? Just leave the past alone," Grace said. "We can't undo it."

Faith got to her feet. "I'm not angry with you anymore, but I was when I left for college. You were bossy and strict and mean all the time. But I was nineteen and I'm not sure I wouldn't have felt the same way about Mom." She slapped at the dust on her hands. "I'm a mother myself and I understand things now that I didn't back then. My boys hate my guts some days."

Hope looked at her hands, then at her sister. "I probably did a terrible job with a lot of things. I was ready to leave home and couldn't. I had a house to keep up, laundry, meals, your homework assignments, and whatever Dad needed. I may have been unprepared for all that responsibility...but I thought I was doing a good job, anyway."

Grace cleared her throat. "You did a *splendid* job. We turned out to be model citizens who can function all on our own. Now, can we finish this inventory and get out of the heat, please?"

Hope stared at her sister a moment. "I guess you remember things differently than I do, Grace. I'm truly sorry that you don't like me much. I'd like that to change, but it's up to you, not me." She turned to Faith. "Since I won't be much help here, I'll go back and tackle more of the files and stuff in the house. If you think I can help with anything, let me know."

Faith turned to Grace when the door closed behind Hope. "Did you have to be so damned sarcastic with her? She loves us very much."

"I just call it like I see it, kiddo. It's the Army way."

Thursday passed much like Tuesday and Wednesday had except there were no visitors to the Blessing homestead. Hope spent most of the day on the road, introduced herself, collected accounts, and solicited new work for the company. She promised their bond was satisfactory and that they would most certainly deliver the goods on time. Two new, though small, clients agreed to fax work orders the following week.

In Tallahassee, she met with the Small Business Administration to discuss the possibility of a loan, only to find out that even if the trucking company had an "A" credit rating, loans were simply not being approved at the present time.

Gathered around the dinner table once again, they decided to celebrate the new customers they'd gained. Grace held up her glass in a toast.

"To slow-but-steady progress, ladies!"

The sisters clinked their glasses and laughed. "Business at the shop is picking up, I hear," Hope offered, stabbing a roasted potato. "Margaret Ann, my shampoo girl, called me today. Quite a few new clients have called for appointments."

"Well, that's good news, too. Maybe all this doom and gloom is finally over," Grace said.

Faith smiled. "You know, I was thinking. If we can't get a loan, maybe we can find a partner with some cash. You know, an investor maybe?"

"Investors usually want to invest in things that are showing a profit. It will be a long time before we can do that," Grace said.

"Maybe not," said Hope, taking a sip of sweet tea. "We could be in the black in six months if we keep bringing in new business."

"You're betting the barn we don't have any setbacks and that's not realistic. We'll have our share, I'm sure. I've seen some of the most foolproof plans in the Corp of Engineers go up in smoke damned quick," said Grace around the spare rib she chewed on. "And that's when no one is out there trying to sabotage you on purpose."

"I'm going to be the optimistic one here, okay?" said Hope. "You can be the realist and I'll just keep praying for God to give us all the good things we need."

Grace sighed. "Hey, go for it, Sis. Far be it from me to try to change you now."

The girls had just showered off another day's worth of dirt and grime, when a cream-colored Cadillac Escalade pulled into the yard. The shop was inventoried and in working order. The trucks were clean and polished and ready to go. Even the house and the yard looked more presentable thanks to Hope's efforts with the shears and the mowing tractor. What a difference a week made.

They heard the car door slam and Faith looked out the dining room window. "It's Highspring."

"What the hell's he want?" Hope muttered from the kitchen.

He knocked on the door. "I come bearing peace offerings. How about dinner?" he asked, opening the door without an invitation. His crooked smile lit up his gray eyes.

"Here's some chicken from The Roost. I've got all the fixin's in the car. Be right back."

"I'll give you a hand," offered Faith, following him out the door.

"If she falls for that man, I'll have to kill her," said Hope, then returned to the kitchen for plates and napkins.

"She won't, Big Sis. She just feels bad because you treat him like dirt and he wants to make up," said Grace.

"Make up? You don't 'make up' after thirty-eight years. You start over maybe, but you don't just go back to the way things were."

"Hope, I know that. We all know that. It's just a figure of speech. That's what I told you yesterday, isn't it? No different with us than it is with you and him, but maybe we all decide to start new. From here?"

Hope looked at Grace. "I don't know. I really, really don't know."

Grace shrugged. "I understand. I don't know, either. But at least we don't have to cook dinner tonight."

"There is that," Hope said with a smile.

The porch door banged and Faith and Eddie dropped boxes of food on the glass-topped table.

"Let's eat," Faith called to her sisters.

Grace and Hope set the table. While everyone piled plates high with biscuits, fried chicken and garlic-laden greens, Eddie asked the women for an update.

Hope and Grace took turns reporting what they'd accomplished in a few short days. Faith ate as though she hadn't eaten in weeks.

"Did you get the bankruptcy paperwork filed?" Grace asked. "We don't need Betty Jo winning this battle because a law clerk missed some deadline."

Eddie half-smiled. "You ladies aren't in the hands of a clerk. We'll file the bankruptcies next week. But I filed the injunction to keep the foreclosure from happening. How many creditors are involved?" he asked.

"The only one is Clark Savings and Loan," Hope said. "I've gone through everything in the office and talked by phone to all of Dad's vendors. Everyone's within thirty days except the bank. Daddy has sixty days on the fuel bills at the Depot and six months with the tire dealer. And he made some partial payments to the bank too, but they only paid the fines and fees, never the principle."

"Well, that makes it easier then. How about taxes? Is Percy paid up on the place?" Eddie asked.

Hope nodded. "I called the county Wednesday and the taxes are paid through last quarter. They'll be due again in another month, but we're not behind. Looks like his sales and income taxes are current to last quarter. I'm telling you, he was paying everything on time except the loans."

By this time, everyone had pushed aside their plates. Lulls in the conversation were filled by the sounds of cicadas and frogs out by the creek.

Eddie studied each woman a moment. "Did you have any luck with Percy's larger contracts?"

Faith shook her head. "Dad was underbid by a company named Mattheson Transport. If they really screw up, we'll get another chance. And, if we're still around, we can bid next year but the contracts are set for this year."

Eddie's face flushed and he got to his feet. "Gads, this just gets smellier by the day. If Craig Mattheson is the owner, then Betty Jo put him up to it. He was husband number two and I thought she took him for everything he had. Maybe she gave some of it back."

Grace glanced at Hope. "Craig Mattheson is the owner, all right. When Hope was in Tallahassee yesterday, she checked the corporate registration."

"Well I'll be damned," Eddie said, sitting again.

"You very well may be," said Hope, smiling over the rim of her tall paper cup. "I told Betty Jo that you would be preventing her from causing the Blessing family any more damage. Now you'll have to face her wrath, too."

He looked her in the eye. "Won't be the first time, will it?"

Chapter Seven

Showdown

Hope woke in total darkness to the shrill ring of the telephone. For a moment, she just sat on the sofa, shaking her head, trying to get her bearings. She glanced at the clock on the bookshelf. The phone kept on ringing.

Who the hell is calling at midnight on a Sunday night?

She got to her feet and stumbled to the desk. "Hello?"

She listened for a minute. "A fire? Erma, are you all right?"

She tugged on her hair with her free hand. "Oh lord, I don't need this right now. Thank you for calling in the fire for me. I'll be there as soon as I can get dressed and get over there."

She listened and paced. "We'll talk when I get there, okay? I'm leaving here in five minutes and should be to your place in fifteen. Thank you, darlin'."

Hope reached for the lamp on the end table in the office and snapped on the light. She dashed upstairs, splashed water on her face and ran a brush through her hair, then grabbed her purse and the truck keys and came back down the stairs at a run.

She slipped into her moccasins at the front door, locked it, then ran to the pickup.

The Faithfully Yours Beauty Salon had gone up in flames an hour ago. Tears ran down Hope's face. The anxiety in her chest sucked the air from her lungs.

"I'm okay," she whispered to the ghostly oaks that swayed in the beams of her headlights. "If someone's trying to kill me, they'll just have to try a little harder."

Hope turned off of Magnolia Road onto Main Street, but she couldn't get to Second because of the fire and emergency vehicles that blocked the road. Across from the Old Tyme Ice Cream Shoppe, she made a left, drove two blocks, made a right, then pulled into the driveway at Erma's house and parked.

Trembling, she got out of the car, but before she could get to the house, Margaret Ann came barreling out the door.

"I'm so sorry. I know how bad things are already, I just can't understand what's going on. After church this morning, I went to the shop, did the floors, and took inventory, but I swear nothing was turned on."

"The only thing that's important is that no one was hurt, do you hear me?"

Erma came out the door and walked along the driveway to join them. In silence the three women watched as the fire fighters wound their hoses back onto the truck reels.

"Is there anything I can do, ladies?" asked a familiar voice. Hope turned to find Reverend Jackson standing just behind them.

"I surely don't know, Reverend, but thanks for offering. I'm praying that we didn't just lose what little we had left."

He put his hand on her shoulder. "I'm sorry, Hope. You've sure got your hands full right now."

She shook her head and held up her hand. "I know, I know. I can hear my father saying it now. 'What doesn't kill you makes you stronger.' Well, by now I should be able to bench press his entire truck fleet."

The reverend chuckled. "Where are your sisters?"

"Faith is in Texas and Grace is in New Mexico. They flew home yesterday to take care of things so they can stay at the farm for a few weeks." Hope glanced at her watch. "They'll be back in about sixteen hours."

Erma shook her head. "Damned shame, honey. I hope for both our sakes, the damage isn't too bad. Of course, maybe I can drum up some business with a fire sale," she said with a grin.

Hope gasped. "Erma, the smoke will have damaged the clothes in your shop. I'm so sorry."

Her friend shrugged. "I'm thankful that I didn't have a wedding gown or special project going on. Like I said, give me a chance to clean out the shop a bit and get ready for the fall inventory. Always a bright side, Hope. Remember that."

"I'm going to walk over and see if I can find out what's happening," Reverend Jackson said.

"I'll go with you," Hope said. "You stay here with Erma," she instructed Margaret.

Shawn Jackson and Hope walked the two blocks to Main Street. Tall palms lined the north side of the street, separating the shops and sidewalks, from the traffic. Hope leaned against the tree closest to the corner and watched the firefighters.

Two of the three fire trucks were just pulling away, though a sheriff's deputy was still speaking with the fire captain. Hope and the reverend crossed the street and waited.

The deputy came to speak with them. "Do you folks know the owners, here?"

"I own the salon. Erma Delacruz owns the dress and tailor shop next door." She looked at the charred and jagged front window that now dripped water.

"I'm sorry, ma'am, I have some questions for you. Where were you when the fire started?"

Reverend Jackson tightened his hold on her arm. "Was this deliberately set, Deputy?" he asked.

"The captain thinks it was. Looks like a wastebasket full of acetone-soaked rags was set on fire near the middle of the store.

Cigarette tossed in there started it right up." He opened his notepad and motioned at Hope. "Your whereabouts, please?"

"I was at my father's house, the Blessing Farm, the other end of Magnolia. One of my employees called, told me there was fire." Hope swallowed. "She saw the flames from her home."

"Why weren't you at the apartment, ma'am?" the deputy asked, fixing his dark gaze on Hope.

"My father just died. My sisters left yesterday for a couple of days and I didn't want to leave his place empty."

"So, no one was with you?" asked the deputy.

Hope nodded. "That's right. I've been staying at Daddy's place since last Saturday. I didn't have anything to do with this."

Shawn pulled her aside by the arm. "Maybe you'd better call Eddie and let him handle this for you. You never know when you're going to say something that makes it all worse, you know."

"I don't have a damned thing to hide and I sure don't need an attorney. If this is arson, maybe someone should talk to Betty Jo who just can't stand the idea that she's not going to steal anything else away from me," Hope said, jerking her arm from the minister's grasp.

"Ma'am, where can we reach you if we have more questions?" asked the deputy.

Hope gave him two phone numbers and the address of the farm. "I'm going to check on my friend and see if we can't all go home and get some rest. You let me know if you need to speak with either of us."

Hope stiffened her back, raised her chin, and marched along the sidewalk back to Erma's house. She knocked on the door and Margaret Ann opened it.

"Come on, I'll walk you home, " Hope said. "Erma, I'll come by tomorrow and see what we can do to help you, okay?"

"I'm not going home," Margaret Ann said. "Erma and I can get an early start on cleanup tomorrow, if I stay here. I guess you won't be needing me at your shop for a while."

"Maybe a few days, but no longer than that. Don't you go getting yourself another job—I don't know what I'd do without my number one shampoo gal!"

Margaret Ann smiled and gave Hope a quick kiss on the cheek. "I'll be ready when you are, for sure. You get home safe, now."

Hope waved goodbye as she walked to the truck, then her cell phone rang.

"Hello?" She placed it on the console, then hit the speaker button. "Hello?"

"Hope? This is Eddie. Are you okay?"

"I'm fine." Hope rolled down the window a few inches. "Madder than a mockingbird that someone could've been hurt, but everyone's okay."

"I'm on my way over. I'll meet you at the farm in a half an hour."

"I don't know who called you, but we're fine, Eddie. I'll talk to you tomorrow about this if I must," she said, turning on to Magnolia Road.

"With Faith and Grace gone, you're a sitting duck. I can sleep on the couch or in my car, but I'm not leaving you alone."

"The Reverend has a big mouth. Guess I'll see you when you get here." Hope sighed.

Then she disconnected the call.

Monday, just after sunrise, Erma, Hope, and Eddie were hard at work clearing debris and water from the beauty shop. The rest of the town slept as they swept ash and glass from the floor and dumped the smelly, mucky mess into a large trash can.

Eddie hammered a large sheet of plywood over the broken plate glass window in the front of the salon. "The cafe will be open at seven, how about I get us all coffee and something to eat?"

Hope kept sweeping and shook her head. "I don't need anything, thanks."

Erma looked at her. "Well, that sounds great, thanks. Guess I'll have a honey biscuit and a large coffee with milk." She put her trash-can to the side and stretched her back. "Hope, you have to eat. You'll be sick if you skip meals and keep working like this."

"I suppose you're right." She looked at Eddie and forced a smile. "Coffee and a sweet roll would be fine, thank you."

"Light and one sugar, right?"

She nodded, and this time the smile was genuine. *He remembered . . . .*

"I'll be back in a few minutes," he said and dashed out the door.

Erma put her hand on Hope's arm. "Are you going to be rude to the guy forever?"

"I might," Hope said.

"Do you want to talk about this, then? It's going to be very hard to move forward if you can't let go of the past."

Hope put her hand on her hip and stared at her friend. "How do I deserve such a good friend?"

"I believe we're at least even on that score." Erma picked up the dust-pan again.

"I hope so," Hope said, sagging into one of the styling chairs. "I was so hurt when Eddie left town because I thought what we had was special. It hurt more than I can say, when I found out that he'd left with Betty Jo."

"But that was a long time ago and you were kids anyway. Besides, he dumped her quick, so how important was she to him, anyway?"

Hope squeezed Emma's hand. "You're right, of course." She picked at the bare spot worn in the arm of the chair. "But Eddie didn't turn around and come back for me. I never left town, so I wasn't hard to find if he'd been looking. You wouldn't think that someone who planned to marry you would just vanish without a word, forever."

"You don't know that he didn't try to contact you. Maybe he did and you just never got the message."

"This isn't Romeo and Juliet, Erma."

Hope stood and picked up a melted comb from the floor. "I'm sure he had his reasons for not coming back. He left town with the home-coming queen whose daddy was rich. I was an idiot to think he really loved me. It was high school foolishness, nothing more. We can't go back and change things anyway. Just more water under the bridge, at this point."

"Glad to hear you feel that way. After all, according to the Bible, water is the sign of redemption, cleansing, and rejuvenation."

"It's also used to drown people," said Hope, retrieving her broom.

Eddie came through the door with a cardboard carrier filled with cups and white bags. "I hope you are not talking about drowning me," he said with a grin.

"The thought never crossed my mind . . . "

Tuesday morning breakfast in the Blessing farmhouse resembled more of a war council than a meal. Eddie had returned to Ocala when Grace and Faith had both arrived back home.

"Look," Grace said, slamming her fork on the table, "Betty Jo's a bully. Bullies back down when they're confronted. We go tell her we're onto her and that fair competition is one thing, but low-balling and sabotage are something else."

"I wouldn't be surprised if she started that fire, either," said Faith. "I can't believe anyone would think that *you* did it."

"If I find out she is responsible for the fire, believe me, I'll make sure she pays one way or the other," said Grace.

Hope waved her hands. "Please calm down. I have no problem setting Betty Jo straight, but I'm just not sure that doing it on her turf is the smartest thing. Maybe we tell her to meet us here."

"And why would Her Highness do that?" Grace asked, wrinkling her nose.

"We could tell her we know what she's doing with Mattheson

Trucking. Maybe she'll come talk to us, then," Faith said, finishing her coffee.

Grace looked at her sisters and shook her head. "You two are something else. Go ahead, see if you can get her to come out here, but if not, I'm going into town, and have it out with her." She pointed at Hope. "This has gotten way out of control as far as I'm concerned."

Hope looked at Faith, who smiled and winked. "I'll call her. After speaking with Beau this weekend, I'm ready for a fight, anyway."

Just as Hope loaded the last of the dishes into the dishwasher, Faith came into the kitchen.

"She said she was told not to step foot on our property. If we want to talk to her, we're going to have to go to the bank."

Hope looked at her sister. "Okay, then we go to the mountain."

She collected Grace from the office and the women all climbed into Hope's truck. Grace drove into town and parked along First Street, in front of the Davis Funeral Home.

"All roads lead back to this place, don't they?" she muttered.

"Now you promise to keep your temper, right?" Faith asked Grace.

Grace scowled at her sister. "I'm just going to lay out the facts, nice and clear. If she doesn't like it, that's her problem, not ours. At least she'll know where we stand."

"No threats, no profanity, and I mean that, girls," said Hope. "I don't want to give her any more ammunition against us."

Like gunfighters at the OK Corral, the three marched up the stone steps and through the door at the Clark Bank and Trust. A few customers stopped what they were doing and watched as Hope walked to the desk outside the mahogany barricade that separated the bank lobby from secured bank areas.

"We'd like to see Betty Jo, please," Hope said, addressing the well-dressed young woman who sat at the desk labeled

"Information."

"May I tell her who's asking for her, ma'am?" she asked, her hand resting on the telephone receiver.

"The Blessing family," Grace said.

The young woman spoke into the phone, then put it down, and stood. "She'll be right down to speak with you."

Faith began to push through the wooden gate. "We'd rather speak to her privately," she said.

"That won't be necessary," a strong voice said from the staircase landing above them. "Whatever you've got to say to me, you can say from there."

Hope looked at Faith and Grace. "I don't like this. Let's go."

"Nope," said Grace, "we came here to talk to the woman, so we're going to talk to her."

"Grace," started Faith. "Hope is right. This won't go well like this."

"Don't care. I'm not going home without saying my piece," Grace said, pushing her sister aside.

"Are you coming down here or are we coming up there?" Grace asked Betty Jo. The bank was so quiet the only sound was the whirling of the large paddle fans rotating above their heads on a long brass pole. Grace put her hands in the front pockets of her jeans. Her light blue sleeveless blouse showed off strong, tanned arms. She was the picture of control—on the outside.

"I suppose you should come up here," Betty Jo said after a long moment.

Faith and Hope trooped up the wooden staircase behind Grace. Betty Jo indicated a large conference room with a table that could easily seat twenty. No one sat.

"So, what's on your little minds?" she asked. "I have a business to run."

"And so do we," said Grace. "A business that was doing well until some strange things started happening. Things like a trucking company named Mattheson, new guys with very light overhead, judging by their rates. And the driver benefits are to die for, aren't they?"

Betty Jo didn't bat an eyelash. "I fail to see what any of this has to do with me."

Faith stepped up. "Rumor has it that you're the backer for Mattheson Trucking and that Craig got his company back when he agreed to do whatever it took to put our father out of business."

Betty Jo's smile was cold enough to bring down the Florida June temperatures to sub-zero. "Your daddy should have taught you not to listen to rumors. They can be so damaging."

"You'd know, wouldn't you? You've spread your share about Amazing Grace, haven't you?" Hope asked, stepping within two feet of her long-time enemy. "And I don't suppose you'd know anything at all about the fire at my beauty salon Sunday night, would you?"

"Of course not," Betty Jo said, moving back a foot. "And if you continue to make these accusations against me, I will sue you for slander in addition to your long list of other legal problems."

Grace moved toward the door and motioned for Hope and Faith to exit as well. She turned and looked at Betty Jo. "Stay out of our way, Betty Jo. We won't stand still for your petty, childish vendettas any longer. Do you understand me?"

Betty Jo's face turned the color of a red Macintosh apple. She sneered. "You have no idea who you are playing with, Grace Blessing."

Pushing both sisters into the hallway, Hope faced Betty Jo. "Don't threaten me or my sisters again, Betty Jo. If you do, it will be the very last time you threaten anyone."

Hope slammed the door and preceded her sisters down the staircase. The four tellers and three customers stood fixed in place as the trio marched through the building and out the door.

Faith nudged Hope as they climbed back into the truck. "What happened to not making threats, Big Sis?" she teased.

"Shut up," said Hope as she buckled her seatbelt. "I should have told her off a long, long time ago."

Chapter Eight

Ties that Bind

Manny Perez left Amazing Grace farm at five o'clock in the morning, in time to watch the gold of a new day color the sky as he drove along I-75. A Wednesday morning with the colleges out of session, the highway was clear sailing for his lumber drop in Ocala and the generator pickup in Chiefland.

At eleven o'clock, he needed to stop for fuel, food, and coffee, so he opted to take SR26 to I-75 in Gainesville. He pulled into Dixie's Place, a favorite stop for truckers whose routes criss-crossed the northern sections of the great state of Florida.

He pushed through the double glass doors and waved at the waitress who wished him a good morning. His first matter of business had been to fill his old International Harvester with diesel fuel. The second, was a trip to the men's room.

He hiked himself onto a red-cushioned, chrome-trimmed stool at the wide, laminated counter and ordered coffee. He placed his empty thermos on the counter as well and the waitress whisked it away to rinse and refill it for him. He stirred a spoon of sugar into his coffee. Then he pulled out his cell phone and beeped Hope's mobile phone.

"Hello, Miss Hope? This is Manny. I'm off the road for some lunch. Mason's lumber yard is done and I'll be getting those generators to the new account in Macclenny in three hours, at the latest. You have anything up that way for me to pick up and bring back?"

His phone chirped when he let off the button. "Nothing yet," Hope said. "Just come on back home after you drop the trailer. We'll pick it up Friday when we go up to the Naval Air Station."

He sipped his coffee and listened. "Okay, I'll be back after six, then. Call me if anything changes." He dropped the phone into the pocket of his neatly pressed gray button-down shirt.

His plate of eggs, grits, and biscuits arrived, steaming hot from the kitchen. He chatted with the waitress who had kids the same age as his.

"James thinks he knows absolutely everything. It's so hard to keep him on the right path," she complained, cleaning the counter around the coffee machine.

"I know what you mean," he replied with a smile. "I keep telling mine that I'm still bigger than he is, so he'd better listen to his mother or I'll have him doing hard labor when I get home."

They laughed and gabbed until she was called into the kitchen. Manny ate more quickly.

"You still driving for Amazing Grace?" someone asked from a few stools to his left.

Manny swallowed the mouthful of cheese grits and nodded. "Good company, no reason not to stay on," he said, looking at the man who'd asked the question.

"They looking for more drivers?" the man asked.

"No idea. Might be. Call them. Speak with Hope or Faith, they're running the shop," Manny said, taking a bite of his eggs and following it with the last of a buttermilk biscuit.

"Heard they were going out of business," the driver

continued.

"Guess you heard wrong," Manny said. "We're missing Percy, but we're doing fine. Lord willing, we'll be hauling freight a long time." He stood, grabbed his thermos, and laid three dollars on the counter for the waitress. He picked up his food slip and turned toward the register.

"Watch the scales up near 301. They're checking weights the next few days," someone called to Manny's back. He waved over his shoulder without turning around. He was more than ready to get back on the road.

He walked to the truck, opened the door and placed the coffee thermos on the driver's seat, then got his long-handled flashlight and began to walk around the truck to check his tires. Bad tire pressure could get a driver hurt and he had no intention of making that mistake, especially when the company was fighting so hard to keep him employed. He circled around the side and rear of the truck, running his hands over the inside and outside tires of the cab and the trailer. When he got to the front of the semi, he sucked in his breath.

"Damn, damn, damn," he said, running his hand through his hair. His rig sat sadly on its two front rims like an athlete with broken ankles. Both front tires were flat.

He examined them slowly, locating the slash in the sidewall of each tire. Repairable, but repairs cost time and money and he couldn't afford to be late with the generators. It was their first delivery for the Davison Feed and Farm Supply.

He called All Roads Truck Repair and arranged for someone to come out and repair the damaged tires, but that meant a two-hour delay at the least.

Then he buzzed the farm. "Manny here. I've got a problem."

Grace was on the other end of the phone. "We don't need problems, buddy. What's up?"

"Someone slashed both of my front tires. I called the tire service, but it's going to be a few hours before I'm on the road."

"Shit," muttered Grace. "Manny, you safe where you are?"

"I'm fine, just mad as hell. I'm going to ask around and find out if anyone saw anything. There was a Mattheson Trucking rig on the far side of the lot when I got here, but it's not here now. Any way you can get me another truck so we can get this trailer of generators delivered on time? Hate to start with a new account and be late."

"Roger that, Manny. I'll bring the Mack over, we'll change the trailer out and you can finish the run to Macclenny. I'll bring your truck back when it's fixed."

"Thanks, Miss Grace. You know where I am?"

"I do. I'll see you in an hour. And Manny, don't do anything stupid, okay? A thousand-dollar tire repair is going to hurt enough. I'd rather not need bail money, too."

Manny smiled and looked at the sky, then made the sign of the cross on his chest. "You just get over here so I can get on the road."

Grace and Faith pulled into Dixie's place and looked around for the blue and white Amazing Grace truck. Faith spotted it parked toward the back of the large blacktopped parking lot. Manny was speaking to another driver, then they shook hands.

Grace maneuvered the Mack alongside Manny's I.H. and shut down the engine. It kicked back with a bit of fuel knock and she waited until it settled down, then she climbed out of the cab.

Faith clamored out of the passenger side door. The two women strode toward Manny, then stopped and waited for him to approach them.

"So what did you find out?" asked Faith, following Grace and Manny around the truck as they unhooked the safety chains and lowered the feet on the front of the trailer so they could drop it away from his truck.

"No one saw anything specific. One of the Con-Way drivers saw someone looking around the truck, but didn't see anything that worried him. No idea who it was, though."

"We know who it was, don't we?" growled Grace, her rawhide-gloved hands on her hips. "This is just plain wrong. Makes it damned hard to keep turning the other cheek, I'll tell you that."

Faith nodded. "Sure does, but we will. We're not going to get sucked into a vendetta game because we'll lose and we'll lose more than the trucks. We've got to get you on the road, Manny," she said, motioning toward her watch.

Manny maneuvered his crippled rig into the open area in the middle of the lot, the hot pavement groaning under the rims and crushed rubber of the front tires. Grace backed the Mack into position and Manny helped her drop the tongue on the fifth wheel plate. They secured the safety chains and checked the tires on the trailer again. He gave them a thumbs up.

"We'll see you at home," Grace said, motioning toward his truck. "You be safe and stay in touch with us, okay?"

Manny nodded and waved, clearly glad to be on his way again. The sisters entered the truck stop and ordered large sweet teas to go. Drinks in hand, they walked back to the disabled cab and leaned against the driver's side running-board.

"So, how bad do you think this can get? Do we have a thousand dollars to pay these guys?" Faith asked.

Grace shrugged. "Dad's account is paid up, so I'm hoping they don't ask me for the money today. If they do, I can pay them. When I went home, I dumped some of my savings into my checking account so I had it available. I'd rather keep it in reserve, though."

"God bless you, sis. I haven't saved anything more than Christmas money in more than fifteen years. I could survive about a month and a half, then I'd be looking at bankruptcy, too," Faith said, chewing on her straw.

"I'm not supporting two growing teenage boys, nor a

daughter and a business and a father. I've never needed much, so I just banked my money. If I'd been more adventurous and invested some of it, we might not be in this position now."

"Don't be silly. You take good care of yourself and that's what you should do."

A black pickup truck pulled off of SR26 and drove down the driveway in their direction. It sported white-trimmed red lettering. Both women stood at attention and Grace reached for her phone.

The driver parked, got out, and walked toward them. Over six feet tall, with dark blond hair streaked with some silver, he held out his hand toward Grace.

"I'm Craig Matheson and I heard you're looking for me." He looked at Grace from head to toe and finally smiled. "Not a lot of foxy ladies looking for me these days," he drawled.

Faith laughed. Grace scowled and let his hand go unshaken.

"What can I do for you ladies?" he asked, the smile gone.

Grace stepped away from the truck and pointed at the two front tires. "You going to pay for these, Mr. Mattheson?" she asked.

He shook his head. "I don't know what you're talking about. I didn't flatten your tires."

"No, of course you didn't. But one of your drivers did. I'd bet the orders came from you," Grace continued.

"Well, you'd lose that bet. I never told any of my people to injure you or your equipment," he said, stuffing his hands in the front pockets of his jeans. He shuffled his scuffed brown cowboy boot-clad feet as he looked around.

Faith looked him in the eye. "Why don't you tell us what you will do for Betty Jo? We know she's behind all this."

Mattheson sighed, pulled his hands from his pockets and ran one through his hair. He looked like a lost puppy dog. "She just about wiped me out in the divorce. I totally understand the concept of pre-nuptial agreements, now. Anyway, about six months ago, she offered to sell me the trucking company back, if I'd agree to her terms. I'm a trucker, ladies. I don't know what else to do with myself. All I wanted was my truck and couple of trailers back. Instead, I have new rigs and some very lucrative contracts."

"What were her terms?" Grace asked.

He shrugged. "I had to make bids that she prepared, to Florida-based companies. And, I had to offer your father's drivers better pay and health benefits. Nothing else regarding your pa's company, I swear."

"Well, maybe some of your drivers are moonlighting, then. Because we have witnesses who saw a Mattheson driver out here by the truck," Grace said, holding his gaze.

He shook his head, his brown eyes clear. "I'm telling you, I don't play that way. I'll see what I can find out for you and we'll prosecute whoever did this, I promise. And he'll never drive in Florida again if I have any say about it."

"We don't want any more trouble. We're going after those contracts again at the end of the term, Mr. Matheson. We won't cheat to get them, but we're going for them."

"Fair enough," he said. "I'm about breaking even on them anyway. I couldn't afford to bid this low another year." The corners of his mouth turned up in a boyish smile. "Call me Craig, will you?"

"I suspect that once Betty Jo is done with us at Amazing Grace, she'll be after your company again. You may not have another year to worry about," Faith said, looking at her sister who nodded in agreement.

Anger flashed in his eyes. "You could be right. Damn that woman, anyway. The world would be a much better place if she weren't in it, I tell you."

Early Thursday morning Erma wheeled out racks of clothes onto the sidewalk. Margaret Ann followed her out with a large sandwich board sign, which read *FIRE SALE TODAY. ALL ITEMS 50% OFF.*

Erma checked her watch. “We’re ready. Just need customers.”

“We need more customers, too.” Margaret Ann stared at the beauty salon like a puppy watches his master get on the school bus in the morning.

“Say,” Erma snapped her fingers. “I have an idea. Be back out in a minute.”

She ran into the dress shop. Five minutes later, she tacked a poster to the plywood covering the salon window. *SHAMPOO & CUT $15 TODAY ONLY* . “There. Now we’re ready!”

Margaret read the sign. “Erma thanks. I hope it helps.”

“Honey if this sale goes right, you’ll have to call in reinforcements.”

“I hope so.”

Two women stopped by, looked through the racks, and purchased six items each.

As Erma rang them up on the cash register, one woman asked, “Is the beauty shop open? It doesn’t look like anyone is in there.”

“Yes, we’re open. Come on over when you’re finished here.” Margaret Ann scurried over to the beauty shop and turned on all the lights. A few minutes later the women followed.

Hope strolled into the salon. “Hey darlin’. Erma filled me in. I think it’s a great idea. If it gets too busy we’ll call in one of the girls.” She proceeded to begin shampooing the next person. Three more women entered, bags in hands from the fire sale next door.

Faith walked in next. “Need a shampoo girl?” she asked, wiggling her fingers in the air.

Hope grinned. “Maybe a little later you can check on us, but we’re okay for now. Could you see if Erma needs help with her sale?”

“Sure. I’ll catch you later,” Faith said, darting back out the door.

She waved to Reverend Jackson who was across the street,

then busied herself helping a woman to find a blouse to match her chocolate-colored skirt.

A moment later, she heard tires screech and an engine rev. She looked up in time to see a silver coupe speeding down the street, headed straight for the reverend. Before Faith could warn him, he'd jumped back and tripping over the curbing, he landed flat on his back, sprawled across the sidewalk. The silver coupe sped away.

"Are you all right?" Faith called from across the street.

Reverend Jackson straightened up and brushed at his trousers. "I'm okay. I was planning to help Erma with her sale."

He looked both ways, then trotted across the deserted street. Faith hugged him. "If you're okay, why are you trembling?"

"You're trembling a little bit, too," he answered.

"Almost getting run down by a car is a little scary, I'll admit. Sure is a lot of strange stuff happening around here."

"Do you want me to call the cops?" Erma asked as she rushed to his side.

"No need for the cops, Erma. Just a freak accident, I guess. Let's get working the sale here. How is it going?"

"Really good. I'm glad you came. Faith and I have been holding down the fort. Hope is busy and we're expecting Grace a little later."

The reverend walked over to Faith. "How are you girls doing with the business?"

"We've had a few setbacks. Like this fire, and some truck tires being slashed, but we'll get by. We have to."

"Why do you think these things are happening?" he asked.

"I truly believe this is Betty Jo's doing." Faith clenched her fists. "I could just beat the tar out of her."

"She is a mean one, that Betty Jo Clark." Reverend Jackson nodded. "As mean as a hungry gator."

His cell phone whistled, alerting him to an incoming text message. "Excuse me a minute, ladies." He walked into Erma's shop, phone in hand.

He read the screen. *I know all about you. You ministers all have your dirty little sins. You need to stop helping those Blessing girls or your days are numbered here.*

Beads of perspiration poured down his face. His hand shook as he turned off his phone and placed it in his pocket, and walked back outside. He wiped his brow with his handkerchief.

"Is something wrong?" Faith asked.

The reverend sat on a folding chair next to her. "Everything is fine. Just a little church matter that needs attention." He patted her hand. "Nothing to worry about. I need to handle something I should have taken care of a long time ago."

Chapter Nine

Gone Missing

Hope sat in the office, entering their new accounts into the computer. While thankful for what sure seemed to be God's blessings on them, she wasn't taking anything for granted. She was working hard not to worry about what might happen next.

Manny and Patrick had both rigs hooked up and on the road by eight o'clock on Friday morning. Patrick was taking the over-the-road runs to Alabama and Tennessee, while Manny was going to make the trip to Key Largo and Naples.

Grace and Faith were in the garage making some badly needed welding repairs to the spare Mack that Percy had owned since 1971, when a green and white Alachua County sheriff's truck pulled into the truck driveway and parked. Hope watched the occupant step down from the SUV and close the door.

She opened the door before he could knock.

"I'm looking for Hope Kane, Grace Blessing, and Faith Walker," he said, consulting a small notebook. His tan blazer fit well over broad shoulders.

"I'm Hope, my sisters are in the garage. What's this about?"

"Let's get your sisters in here so I only have to do this once," he said, moving his six-foot frame out of the doorway to let her pass through.

"What's going on?" asked Grace when they'd assembled in the small office. Hope shrugged.

"My name is Detective Larson. I'm with the Alachua County Sheriff's office. I understand you three have a problem with a Miss Betty Jo Clark. Want to tell me about that?"

Faith sucked in a breath. "What's happened, Detective?"

He ignored Faith and Grace and focused on Hope. "You answer my questions, first. You had words with her Tuesday according to the folks at the bank. Maybe even threatened her. I'm asking for your side of the story. We can talk here, or we can talk at the office in Gainesville. Up to you."

Hope dropped into her chair and folded her hands on top of the desk. "Betty Jo's been on my case since we were seventeen years old. High school rivalry, I guess. We're in bankruptcy proceedings to try and save our homes and businesses. We went to talk to Betty Jo because we found out she's behind some pretty shady stuff concerning our father's estate."

"And you promised she'd be sorry for that, didn't you?" he asked without looking at her.

"I suppose I did. I lost my temper with her, which isn't surprising. She's always been able to push my buttons. But I haven't seen or talked to her since Tuesday, though I truly thought she'd be showing up at the fire sale yesterday."

"Why would she do that?" he asked.

"Just to rub it in. We didn't start the fire and we're pretty sure she had something to do with it." Hope sighed. "Now, why all the questions?"

He ignored her question. Turning to Grace and Faith, he asked, "How about you two? You were there Tuesday. Where've you been since then?"

Grace laughed. "I've been driving part of the time." She gave the officer a brief version of the tire issues they'd suffered on Wednesday. "You can check the police report we filed with the Gainesville PD about the tires. Yesterday, I was here until after two, working on some new racks in the garage. Then I went to town to help with the fire sale."

"I was with Grace on Wednesday when we went to rescue Manny, and I was helping Erma at the dress shop yesterday," Faith said evenly. "Grace joined us around three. Your turn. I don't think we'll answer any more questions until you tell us what you're after." She leaned against the doorjamb and tucked her thumbs in the pockets of her jeans.

Det. Larson closed his notebook and put it in his shirt pocket. "Betty Jo Clark didn't show up for work this morning. She left the bank yesterday at regular time, had a meeting with some investors this morning and missed it. After not finding her at home, her assistant called us about your conversation Tuesday."

"Great," said Hope, "just great. We don't know anything about it, I can promise you that. We're too damned busy trying to keep all the ends from unraveling around here."

"Wait a minute," said Grace, "that woman must have more enemies than Florida has alligators. Hell, she's got a fistful of ex-husbands and ran a third of the business owners out of Merciful, including her own father. I hope we aren't the only people in that little book of yours."

He held Grace's gaze, then reached in his jacket pocket. He tossed a business card on the gray steel desk. "If you hear anything, give me a call."

All the Blessing women were gathered in the office at the house when the clock chimed eight times. Eddie had arrived fifteen minutes earlier.

"I can't believe how consistently worse this situation gets," Eddie said, drumming his fingers on the arm of the overstuffed chair. "I'm not a criminal attorney, so let's hope this doesn't go that far. You three should not have gone to the bank. What were you thinking?"

Grace sipped her bourbon, then put the glass down on the table beside her chair. "We were thinking we'd taken enough crap off that woman and we were giving her notice to cease and desist."

He shook his head. "You told her, all right. You told the whole damned town that if she doesn't back off, you'll take care of her. Now she's disappeared. Just what you needed."

"We didn't do anything to Betty Jo. We don't have anything to worry about," Hope said. "There can't be any evidence to the contrary since we aren't involved."

"Don't be naive, Hope. The justice system is far from perfect," Eddie said.

Faith crossed her feet at the ankle. "She probably disappeared to make it look like we did something to her. Wouldn't put it past her."

"Erma said that she thought the driver of the Mustang that almost ran down the reverend yesterday looked like Betty Jo," Hope said.

Eddie stood straight. "What was that?"

"Yesterday, around eleven o'clock, the reverend was almost run down by a silver Mustang. With his bad leg he doesn't move so fast, but he got out of the way in time," Faith said.

"Anyone report it to the sheriff's office?" Eddie asked.

Faith shrugged. "No idea. Reverend didn't want us fussing about it. We were busy at the sale for hours, then the reverend got a text message from someone. Said he had to take care of some old business for the church."

"Great. You ladies need to have all this stuff documented from now on. Everything that happens gets reported to the authorities. We need to establish a trail. Now, fill me on the rest of the week."

Shortly after ten, Faith and Grace excused themselves to go to bed. Hope and Eddie moved to the back porch to talk. Hope curled up in the corner of the wicker sofa. Eddie settled into a chair.

"I'm worried," Hope said softly. "Up until now, no one's been physically hurt. I've got a bad feeling about this latest development."

Eddie was quiet for a minute. "I'm sorry, Hope."

The ice in the glass clinked as Hope swirled the amber liquid. "You didn't cause this, Eddie. We are the victims of our own negligence and pride," she said.

"I'm not so sure that's true, but I was apologizing for running off with Betty Jo after graduation."

Her laugh was sharper than she intended. "I didn't realize until I saw you again that I really am still hurt. I know it's ancient history." She sighed and forced a smile. "I'm really better with it now than I've ever been. But I'll admit, I'd like to know what happened. Was it me?"

He shook his head and looked at the floor. Then he looked her in the eye. "After I dropped you off at home that night, me and some of the guys went over to the Clark's house. I got drunk, supposedly had sex with her in the back seat of her Impala, and then about two weeks before graduation, she announced she was pregnant. Since I couldn't remember much of anything for sure, I figured the baby was mine, like she led me to believe."

Hope's heart slammed against her chest so hard she was sure it would end up in her drink. She inhaled a deep breath. "Gee, I don't know if I want to hear any more," she said, gulping her drink before cradling it in her lap. "You made love with her! But you'd just told me you loved *me*! How could you?" Hope had told him it was ancient history, but suddenly, it didn't feel so ancient. The hurt was sharp.

"I'm not sure I ever did have sex with her. At least not that night. But even if we did get it on in the back seat of her car, it was not making love!" he said. "I was barely even talking to her when she told me she was pregnant. I couldn't let that baby grow up without a father, though. I didn't have a dad and I couldn't bear the idea that my baby wouldn't know me."

Hope sat silent a long time. When she spoke, it was barely a whisper, but she meant every word. "I'm sorry that you lost the baby, Eddie. Children add an incredible dimension to life."

"We didn't lose the baby, Hope. She was never pregnant. I was a chump. It was a ploy her mother taught her, I'm sure. Underneath the beautiful, mean exterior, Betty Jo is a very insecure woman. Her father's a gentle, laid back man; her mother was a scheming, conniving, social climber. Vicious as they come."

"So, how did she let an attorney son-in-law get away?" Hope asked.

"I was in my third year at the university when I realized, I just couldn't continue on with the charade. Betty Jo was choking the life out of me. I was miserable that I'd hurt you so badly, and I think she knew it and went out of her way to grind salt in the wound." He looked out over the yard between the house and the garage. A coyote cried off in the distance.

"In desperation, I talked it over with Betty Jo's father. He understood my position, though he warned me that her mother would not take it kindly at all. He told me he stayed in his marriage because he was terrified that his wife would wrestle the family bank away from him." Eddie laughed. "Of course, after she died of cancer and he retired, he gave the bank to Betty Jo. Not much difference."

Hope smiled in the darkness. "The difference was choice. And once we've made them, it's best to keep on, I suppose."

"Can you forgive me?" asked Eddie. His question was soft. His body tense. As if her forgiveness truly mattered.

"I'm working on it. Reverend Jackson insisted that I make forgiveness a priority and it seemed like good advice."

The crickets chirped and the cicadas sang along the bank of the river. Hope let Eddie's confession seep into her heart, and she felt something loosen. Something that had been bound tight for years. It was hard to let go. "You never remarried." She needed to move away from her feelings and get back to his.

"Nope," Eddie said after several minutes of silence. "You know, if I could do things over, I'd do them differently, Hope," he said.

She sighed. "That's probably true for most of us, Eddie." She uncurled her legs and got to her feet.

"It's been a long day and a long week. I'm ready for bed."

Eddie stood, reached out to rest his hands on her shoulders. He pulled her to him gently and placed a kiss on her forehead. Letting his hands drop to his side, he stepped back and reached for the handle on the wooden screen door.

Hope almost smiled. "You're not entirely forgiven yet, you

know."

Shawn Jackson paced around the rectory office, clutching a stack of papers. He slammed them face down on the battered, oak desk, slumped down in the leather desk chair, and wept.

He lifted his head at the sound of the door chime, and reached for a tissue to dry his eyes. "Mrs. Higgins," he called to the housekeeper, "tell the caller I'm not receiving guests right now."

"Too late, Rev," said a brusque voice.

Margaret Ann pushed her way into the office, arms clutching brown paper bags. Two plastic bags hung from her wrists. "Have you been hiding from me lately?" She parked herself in a tweed chair in his office. "Rev, you look like a man who just lost his best friend. You called me to pick up a few things for you at the store, and when I arrive you say you're not receiving callers. What's up with that?"

"I'm sorry. I've been working on my sermon." He rubbed his forehead. "I've been very busy with some other things I've neglected." He gathered the scattered papers in a neat pile and slipped them into the top desk drawer.

"I see," Margaret Ann nodded. "Looks to me like you've got as much on your mind as on your desk. Folks are saying that Betty Jo is missing. You want to talk about anything?"

He fumbled with a file folder, not allowing his gaze to meet hers. "No, I'm fine, Margaret Ann, but thank you. And yes, I heard about Betty Jo. She's probably on a jaunt to her house in the Keys. When you're the boss of the business, you can go anywhere you want to, whenever you want to."

She looked at him a long moment and then shrugged. "I guess. I brought you some dinner. A rotisserie chicken, fixin's, and some other food to keep you going. You gotta eat to keep up your strength."

He stood, pulled his wallet from his back pocket, and handed her twenty-five dollars. "Thank you very much – for the food and for worrying about me." He forced a smile. "Maybe say a prayer for me instead of worrying, okay?" He nodded toward the bags. "Just put everything in the fridge. I have a lot of work to finish and I was hoping to get in some fishin' tomorrow." He winced as he lowered himself into his chair.

"Leg still bothering you?" Margaret Ann asked.

"Didn't help falling again yesterday, but it will be okay. I really need to pay better attention to where I'm going, I guess."

"Would seem that way. And, maybe you need to see a doctor." She pointed to his hands. "You're shakin'. Still shook up from that car almost clippin' you yesterday?"

Shawn covered his eyes with his hands and sighed. "Maybe I am still a bit upset. I'll be fine," he said again. He looked at the clock. "Thank you for stopping by, but I do have to get finished here or you won't have a sermon on Sunday."

"I can take a hint." She walked over to him and patted his shoulder. "No need to get up. Rest that leg. I'll just put this food away and let myself out."

The reverend looked up from his desk. "Margaret Ann, wait," he called. "I really appreciate your concern and the food. I don't know what I'd do without your friendship."

"Well, I am concerned about you. That's what friends are for, right?" She smiled. "You get a good meal in you tonight and rest that leg."

"Thanks again. I'll see you Sunday."

"I'll be there," she answered. "I heard the bluegill fishin's good. Hope you catch a bunch."

"What's that racket out there, Caesar?" asked Erma of her old, fat tabby. "I hope it's not those pesky armadillos digging up my garden again."

She moved to the dining room window and raised the shade. "Well, I'll be," she muttered. "Ten o'clock at night and it looks like Reverend is going out of town." She pulled the shade down again and shut off the living room ceiling fan, then the light.

"Well, ain't none of my affair, I guess. Let's get to bed, cat. Tomorrow's the last day of the Fire Sale and we're opening early!"

Chapter Ten

Nobody Knows the Trouble

Patrick Bailey looked forward to getting home next week. In six days, he'd be relaxing in his bass fishing boat, drinking cold beer and pulling in some good-eatin' fish. He was overdue for a few days of bass fishing. He'd damned near missed the entire season, but work came first.

He felt good about his decision to stay on with Percy's daughters. They had their papa's sense of fair play and they seemed like hard workers. Hell, they'd even talked to him about his brother-in-law repainting the truck signs for them. *Things are looking up, yessirree.*

With the Tennessee drops done, he was ahead of schedule. He pulled into his favorite stop outside of Mobile, Alabama, and made a call before he headed inside for a shower, shave, and a chicken-fried steak dinner. Cindy Lou said she was indeed up for some dancing tonight at the American Legion, though she didn't get off work at Sonics until nine.

Freshly shaved and sporting a white polo shirt over his

jeans, he'd polished his Justin boots to a high shine. He was leaning up against the side of the truck with a grin on his face the size of the Arkansas River, when she pulled in to pick him up.

He opened the passenger door on her '68 Camaro and swung his lean frame into the low seat, then leaned over and gave her a kiss.

"Hey, sugar, you're sure looking good," she drawled. "Glad you called me when you did. Boss wanted me to work some overtime and I've already worked near ten extra hours this week."

He ran his fingertip along the line of her jaw. "You know me, baby, always glad to help out a pretty girl."

"I'd better be the only pretty girl you're helping out, Patrick Bailey," she said, her pink-painted lips in a pout.

He tugged on her pony tail and laughed. "No worries. I'm all yours for the next fifteen hours. Let's go."

As Patrick and Cindy Lou pulled out of the truck stop, a black and gold Matheson Trucking rig pulled in and parked beside the locked Amazing Grace truck.

"C'mon, baby," Patrick cooed the next morning around nine. He cranked the diesel engine, all to no avail. Not a click, not a moan, nothing. "Damn," he swore, slamming his hand against the steering wheel.

He jumped down out of the cab and lifted the left engine cover. Everything looked intact. He visually traced the cables to the starter motor, then tugged on them. One came loose in his hand.

"How the heck?" he muttered to himself. Reaching into the cab behind the driver's seat, he pulled out his tool box. In five minutes, he had the cable reattached.

"Everything okay, Irish?" a deep voice asked.

Patrick finished stowing his tools and climbed back out of the truck.

He reached around to shake hands. "I sure hope so, Johnny. Last night everything was fine, this morning she wouldn't start. Starter cable was off."

"Hmm. You have to check that stuff, boy," Johnny said.

"New owners," Patrick said. "Percy's daughters are runnin' the company. Grace Blessing went over this truck herself before putting me on the road. And I did, too. This cable didn't come off by accident."

"Heard some rumblings about Mattheson Trucking being after you folks. Don't sound like Craig's doing, though. He's a good man. I believe one or two of their drivers were in here last night. You didn't hear nothing?" the truck stop owner asked.

Patrick shook his head. "I wasn't here. Had a date, came in this morning."

"Well, Irish, if I were you, I wouldn't leave my rig unattended from now on. Maybe get yourself a partner so's you can watch each other's backs."

Patrick hauled himself into the cab and shut the door. "You might have an idea there, Johnny. Thanks."

The truck started and Patrick sighed with relief. He had a stop in Auburn, Alabama, one in Macon, Georgia and then he was Tallahassee bound. By Monday morning, he'd be back in Florida and only a few hours from that three-day fishing trip.

He'd driven less than thirty miles when the truck started running rough. Then he heard a grinding, tooth-jarring bang, and battled the rig to the shoulder of Interstate 85. Like a dinosaur in the throes of death, it shivered, convulsed, and then rested silently on the roadside.

"Damn it," Patrick shouted. He had a sinking feeling in his stomach. He pulled out his phone, called an old friend, and hoped to God the guy was available. There was no better diesel mechanic this side of the Mississippi River.

The squawk on the workbench made Faith put down the acetylene torch. She picked up the phone and keyed it.

"This is Faith. Over."

"This is Patrick. I'm in Alabama and I've got big trouble. Someone sugared my fuel tank, last night. Over."

She took a deep breath before depressing the mike key. "How many stops do you have left? Over."

"Four. Tennessee's done. I'm sitting in a shop just west of the Georgia border. Still have Peachtree City, Macon and Valdosta in Georgia, then a late delivery in Tallahassee."

"Okay," Faith said. "Stand by and I'll try to reach Grace. She's going to have to bring you another tractor. I'll get right back to you."

"Roger that."

Faith said a quick prayer and clicked the phone to reach Grace. Her sister answered on the third ring. Faith recapped Patrick's call.

"I'm just getting out the shower. Damn it, I should have just stayed in the freaking Corps, already," she grumbled. "At least we got a couple of days off a month. You know, we're fighting an uphill battle on this trucking thing and I'm beginning to think we won't win it."

"Don't talk like that, Grace. We're not gonna get negative about this," Faith chided.

"Well, Miss Positive Energy, pack a bag, because you're going with me," Grace said just before she cut off the call.

Faith put down the phone and began to clean up the shop. The gate she was welding was almost completed, but it was a surprise for Hope. When it was done, she prayed that Hope would understand how much Faith loved and appreciated her.

When she'd left home all those years ago, she'd had no idea what Hope had gone through to try and raise two teenage rebels, but she sure did now.

She dragged the two fifteen-foot sections behind the welding screen and shut off the lights. Grace would be ready to hit the road long before Faith was ready to go.

Worshipers packed the tiny church on Sunday morning. Ceiling paddle fans circulated the air. Every door and window was open to let in the early morning breeze.

"Do you remember Sunday service being this crowded?" Faith whispered.

Grace glanced at her watch and then at the clock on the choir loft. "Can't say I remember what it was like. Except for funerals, I haven't been to a real church service, since, forever. Ask Hope, she'll know."

"Why is it so crowded here today?" Faith asked Hope.

"Our planting season is over for the summer now. That means the farmers have no excuse to not be here with their wives. Doubles the attendance." Hope stood. "I don't know what the holdup is. We never started this late. I'm going to talk to Margaret Ann about it."

Hope walked over to Margaret Ann, Erma and Mrs. Higgins. "What's the hold up?"

"Rev isn't here yet," Margaret Ann said to Hope.

Hope turned to the weekend housekeeper. "Mrs. Higgins, go over to the house and see if he's still asleep." The silver-haired woman scurried out the back door.

"Margaret Ann, why don't you start the music?" Hope said. "If he's sick or something I can lead the service."

As Hope was about to join the choir behind the pulpit, Mrs. Higgins dashed back into the church in tears, her arms motioning for Hope to join her.

"He's not in the house, his bed has not been slept in, and his car is gone. I don't know where he is." She wiped her eyes with a tissue.

Hope patted the woman on the shoulder and looked out at the congregation. "Well, let's get the service done and then figure out what's happened to the reverend."

Margaret Ann seated herself at the organ and set up the sheet music. The organ bellowed out *The Old Rugged Cross*, and the congregation began to sing.

Hope, dressed in a choir robe, processed to the pulpit. "Good Morning, all." She outstretched her arms. "Welcome to our Sunday worship service. In Reverend Jackson's absence, I'll be leading the service today. I'll do my best to fill in for him."

By the time the offering had been collected and Margaret Ann had played the last note of the closing hymn, Hope's nerves were on high alert.

An usher stood by the steps of the pulpit with the day's collection in a beige cloth bag. "Is the Reverend all right?" he whispered to her.

"He had to leave rather unexpectedly on Friday. I'm sure he'll be back in a day or two." *God forgive me for stretching the truth*, Hope prayed with a smile on her face.

At the end of the service, Hope, Margaret Ann, and Erma gathered outside the church to greet the parishioners.

"Give the reverend my best," someone shouted.

"Nice job filling in, ladies," said someone else.

"Where's the Reverend?" Faith asked, when she and Grace joined them outside.

"No idea," Hope whispered.

After the crowd dispersed, the sisters, Margaret Ann, Mrs. Higgins, and Erma met in the vestibule.

"So what happened?" Grace asked.

"We don't know where he is," Margaret Ann muttered.

"I saw him get into his car late on Friday night. He was putting grocery bags and his fishing gear in the car." Erma said.

"I brought him groceries on Friday night. I brought him dinner and a few other things to eat." Margaret Ann turned to Mrs. Higgins. "Did he eat the food I brought?"

"I left for the night about seven. I set out a plate and utensils on the kitchen table." Mrs. Higgins replied. "I asked what he wanted me to take out for him to eat. He said he would get it himself and told me to go home for the evening. So I left."

"Did you see him yesterday?" Grace asked.

The housekeeper shook her head. "I just thought he had early visiting calls, that's all." Mrs. Higgins shook her index finger. "But you know he's been distracted about something the past few weeks."

"He has been trying to help us out with our business problems," Hope said.

"It's not like him to miss a Sunday Service,' Erma said. "I was busy at the shop yesterday, but I don't remember seeing his car when I got home."

"I leave at noon on Saturdays," said Mrs. Higgins.

"He was limpin' bad Friday night," Margaret Ann said. "At one point he grabbed his knee and winced in pain. I told him to get it checked out. He said he would."

"Maybe he checked into a hospital," Faith said. "Maybe the pain got so bad that he called the first aid squad."

"He would have let me know," Mrs. Higgins said.

"It could have happened quickly. And maybe he hasn't had a chance to call."

"But where would his car be?" Margaret Ann asked.

"Maybe one of the paramedics drove it for him, so he would

have a way home," Faith said. "Let's call the local hospitals."

Hope shook her head. "I'm not sure they'll tell you anything but you can try. First Betty Jo is missing. Now Shawn Jackson is gone. I don't know what the connection is, but as Mamma would say, 'I smell a skunk in the woodpile.'"

Chapter Eleven

Turning Up

I'm losing my mind.

With both Betty Jo and the pastor going missing right on the heels of burying her father, Hope was sleep-deprived and tear-prone. Neither the biologically-induced insanity of menopause, nor the call about her husband being found dead in Betty Jo's bed had pushed her so close to the edge of running away and never coming back.

It was no comfort that Grace and Faith had been forced to drive the old Mack to Alabama to rescue Patrick on Saturday, especially since they hadn't gotten back home until nearly one o'clock this morning. In a rental car. The Blessing girls were leaking money they didn't have, like a canoe used for target practice.

That's why she was awake and pacing the back porch, coffee in hand, at seven o'clock in the morning. She'd been awake since four, just long enough to decide that she'd had all the pushing around she was going to take.

She marched out to the garage office and let herself in. The smell of oil and diesel felt like home, maybe even more so than the old wood and pine cleaner smells in the farmhouse. For forty of her fifty-six years, she'd spent a lot of time in this garage. The garage was her father. *Maybe that's why I want to save it so desperately*. But her father was gone—maybe it really was time to just let go.

She went into the office, picked up the phone, punched in the number, and set the cordless on the desk. She clicked on a new digital recorder at the same time she hit the speaker button on the phone.

"Mattheson Trucking, can I help you?" a sweet young voice answered. Hope breathed deep. *Get more flies with honey . . . .*

"I'd like to speak with Craig Mattheson, please."

"He's in a meetin'. He can call you back, maybe," the young thing informed her.

"Sweetie, my name is Hope Blessing. I know it's Monday and I know he's busy, but I want to speak with your boss right now. If I can't speak with him now, please tell him my attorney will be calling him before noon." *Maybe that will induce Mattheson to come to the phone.*

"Just a minute." She put Hope on hold, which thankfully did not include that awful canned music filling the air.

She took another sip of coffee before she picked up the repair estimate for Patrick's rig. She rested her hand over a churning stomach and wondered about the pounding in her head.

"Mattheson," boomed a voice. The recorder blinked to indicate it was activated.

"This is Hope Blessing. You've been sabotaging my rigs and I expect you to pay for all the repairs. In addition, I expect you to stop it immediately." She shook hard enough to all but collapse in the creaky chair behind the desk.

"Miss Blessing, hold on a minute. I'm in my office with an investigator from the Florida Department of Law Enforcement. I'm putting you on speaker with us, so we can discuss this."

Several clicks later, Hope heard another voice in the background. Craig came back on the call. "FDLE's been contacted by the Alabama State Police regarding your truck in Selma, and Gainesville PD stopped by to see me yesterday about the tires. All I can say is that I didn't have anything to do with either incident."

The fact that the law was already breathing down his neck took some of the rage out of her. "It has to stop and it has to stop now. It isn't just coincidence that your drivers show up just before I have a major repair on my hands."

"It isn't, Miss Blessing," another voice stated. "Alabama got prints on your rig that don't belong to your driver. And there's a credible witness, a court clerk on his way home after a long day–lives just up the road from the truck stop. We don't have anything but conjecture to go on with the tire slashing but I promise you, we're working on it."

"Who's going to pay for this stuff, Craig? We don't have the money to keep doing this and you know it. Did Betty Jo put you up to all this?" Hope leaned back in the chair and almost fell out of it, slamming her knee on the desk in an attempt to keep from landing on her butt on the floor. *Hells bells, already.*

"I've told you, the FDLE, the Alabama State Police, and the Gainesville Police Department, that I have nothing to do with sabotaging your rigs. However, I promise you, if that print comes back belonging to one of my drivers, I'll help you prosecute him. You have my word."

"Miss Blessing, please leave this to us to unravel. We'll be in touch with our findings. In the mean time, I recommend that you and your drivers either stay off the roads, or adopt a buddy system and don't take chances. My name is Sgt. McCafferty. Here's my cell phone number in case you need to contact me directly."

She wrote down the number, dictated it back to him to double check it, and ended the call. She glanced at the clock and yelped. *Shoot!*

She was due in Merciful in ten minutes, still had to call Eddie, and her car was running on empty.

Yes, I am going to lose my mind.

The up-side to the day was that the beauty shop was closed for business on Mondays. In addition to losing most of the morning on the call with Mattheson and a call to Eddie, the day was rapidly vaporizing before her eyes. The contractor was due to put in the new plate glass window on the shop and Hope was already twenty minutes late when she got to the gas station. Thank God for Erma and her big heart because she was willing to let the contractor in so he could get started while Hope made her way into town.

She pulled into the Quiki-Mart out on State Road 441, filled the car with gas, then went into the store. “Large coffee and a sweet roll, please.”

“Toasted, ma’am?” the teen clerk asked.

“Yup, toasted and coffee black.”

The clerk poured the coffee and popped the sweet roll in the toaster oven. “Hear about the drowning at Orange Lake this morning?”

“Drowning?” Hope cleared her throat. “What are you talking about?”

He pointed to the small TV screen overhead.

“Let’s go to Orange Lake for a live report,” the local anchor said.

The camera panned the lake area. “A fisherman got the surprise of his life early this morning, when he snagged his line on a body that had washed up under the lily pads. The Sheriff’s office is withholding the identity until the next of kin has been notified,” the public relations officer told the reporter.

“Ma’am? Ma’am?” the clerk repeated, trying to get Hope’s attention. “Here’s your order.” He placed the bag and coffee cup on the counter in front of her.

With her gaze still glued to the TV screen, she reached

for her purse to pay the bill, but she couldn't seem to get her hands to work. *Had they found a man or a woman?*

"How . . . how much?" Her throat felt as though she had just swallowed a large lump of bread dough.

"That'll be three dollars and fifty cents," the clerk said. "Are you all right? You seem a little shaken."

"I'm okay. Just a bit shocked at the newscast, that's all." Hope paid the check, scurried out of the Quiki-Mart, and drove toward the shop, pushing the speed limit the whole way. Her hands shook on the steering wheel and she had to concentrate to get a deep breath, her chest was so tight.

Is it Betty Jo or Shawn? Could there be more people missing than the two I know? And if it is one of them, where is the other one?

At the Faithfully Yours Salon, she grabbed her coffee and roll, and almost ran smack into the broad chest of the glass contractor when she dashed through the back door.

"Hello," she said in a rush. "I'm sorry I'm late. Thank you for coming out to fix this so fast. If you don't need me, I'm going to drop in next door and see Erma."

"Oh, if she's the lady who let me in, she said to tell you that she had to go to the church. She'll be back when she can."

Without waiting for a response, the burly man eased back through the doorway and resumed the removal of the plywood that covered the front of the shop.

Had they heard something about the reverend? Breakfast forgotten, she grabbed her purse and just about jogged the two blocks to the church. She was almost to the front door of the rectory when she realized that the Reverend's Ford Focus was still absent.

Before she could knock on the door, it opened, and Margaret Ann reached out, grabbed Hope by the arm, and pulled her into the foyer. She dragged Hope to the kitchen where Erma sat, her hands clutched her lap.

"Any word from Shawn yet?" Or was he the floater who'd

been pulled from Orange Lake?

"I haven't heard a single word and I'm worried sick. This just isn't like him. He's never done anything like this before. I don't understand at all." Margaret Ann walked to the stove and put a fire under the aluminum coffee pot.

Hope sat in the chair across from Erma and peered into her worried face. "You sure you have no idea why he never showed up for church yesterday?"

Erma and Margaret Ann looked at each other like Faith and Grace used to when they'd just done something wrong. Erma shook her head.

"I've been thinking about it all night. I saw him put his tackle box and poles in the car. I thought it a bit odd he was leaving after dark, but he loves to fish. I just thought he was getting away after losing Percy. You know they were close. But Mrs. Higgins said he was home Saturday morning, at least until noon."

"Well, I am absolutely terrified that he may be the dead person they fished out of Orange Lake this morning."

Erma's face went white. "What are you talking about?"

Hope told them what she'd seen on the television at the Quiki-Mart. Margaret Ann and Erma were as speechless as she'd been when she saw the newscast.

"Lordy, no." Margaret Ann started to cry. "Could be the Reverend or could be Betty Jo. Either way, this ain't good."

Despite her attempts to calm Margaret Ann, the woman was almost hysterical. Hope went to the study and gathered up all the phone books.

"I've got to get back to the store and check on the new frot window," she told the ladies after they'd sipped coffee in the kitchen for almost an hour. "Let's see if we can find him. If he had an accident of some sort, he may be in a hospital or, worse, in a morgue somewhere. Anyone know his favorite fishing spots?"

Both women looked at her wide-eyed. Margaret Ann shook

her head. "I'm not sure, but I think he had a cabin up around Orange Lake. Might be some other lake though, there's so many in that area."

"Well, we can't just sit here and wait to find out who they fished out of the lake. Margaret Ann, why don't you call the hospitals in the Gainesville and Ocala areas? Ask them for anyone who may have been brought in with injuries in the past three days. If we don't find him, we call the Sheriff's office and report him missing."

Hope stood and washed her coffee cup at the sink, then placed it in the dish rack and dried her hands on the dish towel.

Erma stood to leave, too. "I'll walk up to the shop with you. I've got work to do, too. I'm going to redo that front window and today's a good day to get that done." She turned to look at Margaret Ann. "Are you going to be all right or do you want me to stay?"

She managed a tired, red-eyed smile. "I'll make the calls and let you know what I find out. It'll give me something to do besides worry."

Erma and Hope gave her a hug, said their goodbyes, then let themselves out. As they walked up the sidewalk toward Main Street, both seemed lost in their own thoughts.

Hope needed to call her sisters at some point, but knowing how tired they were, figured her conjecture and concerns could wait until dinner time.

"You really think the dead person is the reverend, don't you, Hope?"

She shook her head. "I don't know what to think. I guess the truth is that I'm terrified it will be Betty Jo. That damned detective will be back and I'm not sure any of my family have alibis that will prevent us from being arrested."

"Does Eddie know about all this?" Erma smoothed a length of silver hair that had escaped the bun at the back of her head.

"He knows about the detective's visit when Betty Jo went

missing. I haven't talked to him today. He'd probably tell me I'm worrying for nothing."

They crossed the street together and stood gazing at the brand-new window that sat on the sidewalk outside the salon. Hope breathed a sigh of relief. Even the painted signs on the window were fresh and wonderful, the lettering done in a simple black and gold that stood out in the mirrored frame. *Thank the Lord for fire insurance.*

"Maybe we are, " Erma said, patting Hope on the shoulder. "That window is gonna look great. Maybe I should get mine redone, now. Looks sort of tired next to yours." She forced a worried smile and unlocked her door. With a wave, she was gone.

Hope went through the shop to lock her purse in the office and found Eddie sitting behind her desk, not looking very happy.

The window installation man appeared in the doorway. "We'll have that window framed in shortly. We'll finish cleaning up inside the store, then if you'll inspect it and sign off, we'll be on our way."

"I'll be in the office or upstairs, just let me know when you're ready for me." She glanced at the pile of mail in the middle of her desk, then looked at Eddie. "So, this can't be good news. What brings you here?"

The contractor's work was in high gear. Power tools riveted the window frame in place as Hope's teeth chattered in rhythm with the banging.

"Can we go someplace a little quieter?" Eddie asked.

Keys in hand, she pointed upward. "The apartment will be a little better. Follow me."

They walked out the back door and up the flight of stairs to her apartment. She unlocked the door and left it open behind her. She heard Eddie close it.

He fanned himself with his hand. "It's stuffy up here."

She walked over to the air conditioning unit mounted in

the front wall and turned it on high, then turned on the ceiling fan.

"Better?" She tossed her keys on the coffee table and dropped onto the sofa.

Eddie sat in the high back chair facing her and looked at his hands which were resting on his knees. "I have some disturbing news for you."

"The expression on your face told me I wasn't going to like the reason for your visit. What's wrong?"

"Betty Jo's body washed up in Lake Orange early this morning."

"My God." She covered her mouth with her hand. "I saw the newscast at the Quiki-Mart on my way into town. I thought—I was afraid—it was Shawn."

"Why would you think it was him?"

"He missed Sunday services and I was worried about him, that's all. He left Friday night and hasn't been seen since." She rubbed her hands over her face and got to her feet. "I can't believe it was Betty Jo."

He grabbed her hand. "Do you know what this could mean for you, Hope?"

"The albatross around my neck is no longer strangling me?"

"Very funny. But I'm dead serious. It means that you are the most likely suspect in a possible homicide."

She felt the color go out of her face and her legs felt like rubber. She collapsed into the desk chair. "Oh Lord, I just don't need this right now. I don't need this at all." Hope pulled her hand from Eddie's grasp and covered her face. Tears streamed through her fingers.

"We'll get through this, Hope. I promise we'll get it sorted out." Eddie's voice was soft but determined.

Hope's cell phone danced on the desk beside her keys. Eddie reached forward to the coffee table and picked it up. "Want me to answer this?"

Hope nodded.

"Hello?" Eddie frowned. "It's Eddie. She's right here. Can I give her a message?"

He listened, thanked the caller, and closed Hope's phone. She dropped her hands and sat waiting for the next round of bad news.

"That was Margaret Ann. Shands-Gainesville called the rectory. Shawn Jackson's been there since Sunday morning. He was found beaten unconscious on a fishing dock on Orange Lake."

Chapter Twelve

Worrying

Hope and Eddie sat in her apartment in silence. The soft rumbling of the air conditioner was the only sound in the room. After ten minutes or so, she stood and walked into the kitchen, looking for anything that would give her some breathing space.

"Why on earth was Betty Jo found floating in the same lake where Shawn was found unconscious? What the hell is going on? None of this makes any sense."

"I don't have any answers, Hope. But you need to be prepared. If the State Attorney does come after you, you need to be ready."

"Want a glass of tea?"

Eddie leaned against the doorjamb to the small kitchen. "No. I don't need any tea. Now turn around and pay attention. I'm trying to help here and you need to listen. I'm going to call my friend Jack Edwards and leave him a message. He's a damned good criminal attorney."

Hope fought back tears. "You know, I just can't believe this is my life. I've survived some pretty ugly events in my time, but this just keeps getting worse by the day." She opened the refrigerator door, then closed it again. "I can't afford another attorney, Eddie. Would I qualify for a public defender?"

"You might, but more likely as a business owner, you won't. Even if you did, you get whoever the court appoints to take the case. We could be talking about murder charges, Hope. I wouldn't play roulette with this."

"I don't want to owe you, Eddie. I absolutely hate the idea that I already owe you for all this bankruptcy stuff. I'm fifty-six years old, I should be able to take care of myself financially by now."

He stayed where he was and watched her slump into a chair at the table for two. "More than sixty percent of the country is in financial difficulty right now and more than eighty percent of those people are older than fifty-five." He cleared his throat. "Besides, I don't consider my helping you a debt."

She jumped to her feet. "Listen to me. Lord help me, but I need to deal in the here and now, Eddie. I can't live in the past or keep mourning what we didn't have, so you don't owe me anything. Got it? You do legal work for my family, we owe you for it until Dad's insurance money comes in. But the criminal stuff, I have no way to pay those kinds of bills and I'm not okay with you paying them."

"You're too damned proud, Hope. You've always been too damned proud. Tell you what then. Depending on what Jack can do for you, I'll keep track and you can consider it a loan if it's so damned important to you."

Could she trust him this time around? He seemed so much like the patient and tender young man of her youth, but was she seeing who he was or who she wanted him to be? Her head throbbed. Dread squeezed her chest until it felt like her next breath wouldn't happen. She slumped into the kitchen chair again and hugged herself. She forced herself to relax. Sucked a deep steadying breath into her constricted lungs, rubbed her temples in an effort to banish the headache, then looked up at

Eddie.

"I guess I can live with that if I have to. But he deals with me, not you. Okay? I appreciate the introduction and the loan, I really do, but I need you to focus on keeping Amazing Grace Trucking and the Blessing properties out of the hands of the bank."

She watched him fight a smile before he nodded. He was smart enough not to say a single word. *I always appreciated that about Eddie.*

"How is Margaret Ann? Is she very upset?"

Eddie uncrossed his feet and pushed off the doorjamb to join Hope at the table. "Sounded relieved, I think. At least you all know where he is, right?"

"That's about all we know. Did she say anything about his condition?"

"They didn't give her any other information, just asked her for next of kin information."

"I don't know that Shawn has any surviving kin. His father died in Folsom prison when Shawn was in his twenties."

"I know, but I can get into the hospital to see him. I did some work for him a couple of years ago. As his attorney, I can go see him." He stood and walked to the door. "Jack will call you tomorrow. Go see him and get yourself a counsel of record. It will make life much easier for you."

Wishing it were just another normal day and that she'd had more than a few scraps of sleep the night before, Hope opened her shop for business on Wednesday morning as usual. By eleven o'clock, she had a perm cooking under dryer number one, while she did a hair cut in the first chair. Margaret Ann was due in at noon.

Amazing Grace was two days into a completely uneventful spell. Her sisters were back at the farm. With Manny and Patrick riding together, that left the company with two rigs not running, but the jobs so far had paid well and without any new catastrophes to compensate for, Hope was beginning to believe that pulling out of her financial spiral might be something they'd accomplish. But the clock was ticking. Would her sisters stay past the thirty days if she needed them? Would she be able to ask them to do it? Cautiously optimistic, she didn't quite believe that the worst was over yet.

She finished the cut and rang out the customer, just as the kitchen timer clanged.

"Okay, Mrs. Murphy, let's get that perm washed out." She shut off the hair dryer and moved the small woman to the sink. Donning latex gloves, Hope set the water to warm and began to rinse the solution from the hair, something she'd done a thousand times since she'd gotten her beautician's license back in 1986. "Water's not too hot?"

"No, it's just right. Just like always, Hope."

Nothing is just like always. The Sheriff's office hadn't been by to see her again, but it felt like waiting for the other shoe to drop. She'd officially hired Jack Edwards as her criminal defense attorney. The idea made her laugh and shudder at the same time. Two weeks ago, church-going, minister-marrying, goodie-two-shoes Hope Blessing-Kane would be about as likely to need a defense attorney as Mother Theresa. Now, she was heading for double bankruptcy and murder charges.

"Ouch," cried Mrs. Murphy when Hope yanked her hair.

"I'm so sorry." Hope gulped. *Focus, woman!* She reached for a towel. "I think we've got all this washed out. Let's get you set and dried and on your way."

"Is everything all right, dear?"

Hope smiled, but looked away. "The fire still has me upset, I guess, but I'm fine. I'm sorry I pulled your hair." She gently rubbed with the towel. "Do you like the new window?"

"Very stylish, indeed. That's what this town needs, you know. A little updating and a little more style."

"Well, thank you. Erma's thinking of doing a new window for the dress shop, too. We love our small town, you know, but some fresh paint doesn't hurt anything."

"Some fresh blood would help, too. I know it's awful to speak ill of the dead, but that Betty Jo Clark being gone is a good thing for this town. She was an evil woman, that one."

"I don't know about evil, but everyone knows she wasn't my best friend."

Mrs. Murphy barked a rusty laugh. "Bless your heart darlin', that's about the biggest understatement I've heard in years. If she'd been sleeping with my husband, I'd have made her into gator bait long before now."

Hope fought a smile, reached to her cart, and palmed another curler. "Well, my husband made his bed and seems that God left him in it. Matt betrayed me, not Betty Jo." *I just can't stand her for a hundred other reasons . . . .*

"Yes well, I saw you Monday with a very nice-looking man. Lovely car, too. Was he the insurance adjuster?"

Hope continued to wrap the silky silver strands around the small, yellow curlers. The downside to her business was the gossip. There was no way to duck it and if she had to keep it up, she might be sick. She took a deep breath.

"Believe it or not, that was Eddie Highspring. After all these years, can you believe it? He's an attorney and he's handling my father's estate."

"Highspring. Highspring. Didn't he marry Betty Jo when you graduated high school? I think I remember something about that."

Oh, crap already. Hope finished the last curler and wiped her hands on her smock. "Yes ma'am, it was a long time ago but there's nothing wrong with your memory. Let me get you a cup of coffee and tuck you back under that dryer." *And I won't have to talk about this anymore, thank you very much.*

Hope didn't have time to worry about Mrs. Murphy or the memories associated with Eddie Highspring. Before the dryer shut off, Hope had two more customers and Margaret Ann was late.

Lord, I hope she hasn't disappeared now, too.

Eddie's Cadillac was sitting in the driveway down by the truck garages when Hope turned into the drive to the house. *God, please let this be good news for a change.*

She grabbed her purse and the gallon of milk she'd picked up on the way home, and went inside. If Eddie was there to see her, he could come to the house.

She'd put ribs in the slow cooker before she'd left for work that morning and the kitchen smelled like smoky barbeque sauce and tangy vinegar. She lifted the lid, stirred it around, then turned off the cooker.

By the time Eddie, Faith and Grace paraded in, Hope had potato salad made, ribs on a platter, and was microwaving green beans. She tried to ignore the fact that Eddie would apparently be staying for dinner. These days, his appearance meant troubles for her. Damn, she didn't need any more.

"Hey, Sis, smells great." Faith went to the cupboard and lifted out plates, then reached into the drawer to pull out the silverware.

Grace carried the food into the dining room, while Eddie eased the cork out of a bottle of wine.

Hope pulled wineglasses from her mother's china cabinet and placed them on the table. Grace pushed through the swinging door with a pitcher of ice water.

"We ready to eat?" Grace looked around the table. Everyone nodded and sat down.

"Thank you Lord for this food which we are about to receive and bless the hands that prepared it for us. Amen." Faith winked at Hope, then reached for the platter of ribs.

"So," Hope started, sending the bowl of potato salad to Eddie who sat to her left, "what brings you back here so soon? Jack called me before I left the shop to tell me there's nothing to report."

"I went out to the hospital to see what I could find out

about Shawn, today. He's still in a coma. Doctor says his blood pressure is still too low and his skull was fractured. He could come around tomorrow or next week."

Hope shivered. "Or not at all." She spooned green beans on her plate and passed the bowl. "I wonder if the person who hurt Shawn also hurt Betty Jo? Is there any more information on what happened to her? I mean do we even know for sure that it was foul play involved in her death?"

"I have the same questions, you do," Eddie said, sinking his teeth into a rib that proceeded to fall off the bone. It landed on his plate splattering sauce on his tie, but he appeared not to care. "Great ribs, by the way."

"Thanks, but I had help. Margaret Ann's brother butchered a hog last year and sent them over. Mom's recipe made them tasty."

"Speaking of Margaret Ann, how's she holding up?" Faith asked.

Hope sighed. "She showed up at the salon an hour late today, but at least she got there. She'd been cleaning the reverend's house and lost track of time. She's going to cook a few meals tomorrow and stash them in his freezer so he has easy meals when he comes home. But she's worried about him."

Eddie looked at her. "Anything I should know about?"

"Don't think so. His leaving like that without a note or a call has her worried that's all. Out of character for Shawn. Lord knows, he always puts everyone else first. He'd never upset her deliberately."

Eddie finished his ribs, wiped sauce off his fingers and started in on his potato salad. "He was just going fishing for a few hours, probably planned to be back before anyone missed him. Sometimes a man needs time alone, even a man of the cloth."

Grace picked up her wineglass. "With all the crap he has to listen to, fishing time is probably *more* important for him than that average guy."

"Probably right," agreed Faith. "I'll do the clean up tonight. We had a pretty easy day in the shop today, but you look beat," she said, looking at Hope.

Hope smiled. "Thanks, honey. I was busy which is good of course, but Dixie won't be in until tomorrow, so that left me a bit short handed."

"You need help tomorrow? I could clean up and handle the register for you, at least," Faith offered.

"Thanks for the offer, but I think I've got tomorrow handled." Hope turned to Eddie. "Can I go see Shawn in the hospital?"

"Not much to do there right now. I have to check with the sheriff and find out when I can go get his car. As soon as the hospital lets me know he's regained consciousness, we'll go up, okay? Can you get away from the salon on short notice?"

"Dixie will be in the rest of the week. I'll work it out. I just want to make sure he's all right."

Eddie pushed back his chair and stood. "That was delicious. Thanks. I hate to eat and run, but I've got to get going. I'll stay in touch. You get some sleep and I'll call you tomorrow."

Hope got to her feet and walked with him to the back porch door. "You could have called me today and saved yourself the trip out here, you know."

He pushed a loose strand of Hope's hair behind her ear, then let his hand drop. "I know. But I'm worried about you. This worked better for me."

He pushed open the screen door and stepped out. A moment later, he disappeared around the house toward his car. Hope stood there until long after the sound of his car had faded away.

Worked better for me, too.

Chapter Thirteen

Choices

Grace had just poured her second cup of coffee when the phone rang. *Who in their right mind calls a business office before zero eight hundred hours?*

She hit the speaker button on the phone. "Amazing Grace Trucking. Can I help you?"

"Looking for Hope Blessing. Is she around?"

"This is Grace. Can I take a message for Hope?" She set down her coffee and reached for a pen.

"Grace? You gals all sound alike to me, I swear." The deep voice laughed, and Grace knew who the caller was.

"Craig Mattheson. What do *you* want with *my* sister?"

"Hold on, Grace. I was calling to see if there's anything I can do to help you ladies, that's all. I told her and I'll tell you, I had nothing to do with the damage to your trucks. If you need to borrow a rig or my drivers, I'll make sure you get 'em. Your daddy was a damned good man."

"Yes, he was. Are you serious about this help thing?"

"Wouldn't have offered if I wasn't."

"You available to ride shotgun with me later today, then? Since the sabotage, we're riding doubles. I don't want to leave Hope here alone, so I'd rather not take Faith with me."

"Hang on a minute and I'll be right back. Gotta check something first."

Grace sat back in the chair, swung her booted feet onto the desk, and drank her coffee. *Let's see what you're really made of, Craig Mattheson . . . .*

He came back on the line. "Grace, where you going and what time should I meet you?"

Hot damn! Grace cleared her throat and wiped the smile off of her face. "I'll tell you where we're going when we're on the road. In the meantime, you meet me at Annie's off highway 75 at two this afternoon. If we don't have any trouble, I'll have you back there no later than this time tomorrow."

"I'll be there. Maybe we'll get lucky and catch this loser ourselves." She could hear the smile in his voice.

Grace hung up the phone with a smile of her own. *We might get lucky indeed!* Now to break the news to her sister . . . .

"Yes, I know it's too early to count my chickens, but I'm still thankful that things have been calm for a change," Hope told Grace when she called at nine.

"You be thankful, I'll be careful, how's that?"

Hope sighed. "That works. What's up? Will Manny and Patrick be back in time to make the run to Tallahassee today?"

"No, I'm going to do it. Craig called this morning and offered to help us out, so I told him he could ride shotgun with me and he agreed."

"I don't like this, Grace. You could be putting the fox right into the henhouse."

Grace laughed. "Then I'll shoot him, dump him on the side of the road, and our troubles are over."

"Don't even joke about that! One Blessing suspected of murder is more than we need, thank you. Are you sure you'll be safe with him? I agree he doesn't sound like he's involved, but what the heck do we really know about him aside from he was married to Betty Jo and lost everything?"

"Since he's been shafted by Betty Jo then we all have something in common, now don't we? And we know he had the good sense to leave her behind, even though it meant losing everything. I'm going with this, Sis. Be back tomorrow. I'll check in tonight by phone."

Hope walked outside the shop and dropped into a wooden high-back rocker. Erma was already outside of her shop, rocking, crochet needles clicking softly.

The late June rain was gentle, but steady. The women rocked in silence on the wooden porch. Hope remembered other days when she and her sisters had sat on the porch at home and just listened to the rain on the tin roof. Her heart still hurt over the sudden death of her father, but she loved having her sisters with her again. She wasn't sure they shared the sentiment, but they'd managed together for almost three weeks without a serious argument. *That's a good sign, right? I'll bet you're watching, aren't you, Daddy?*

Hope glanced at her watch and got to her feet. "I've got a customer due in a few minutes. I'm going inside and get ready for her. You have a terrific Friday, you hear?"

"Will do, Hope. I'll see you in church, Sunday." Erma waved and Hope shut the door behind her.

Both Hope and Dixie had clients under the hair dryers and one in the chair when the phone rang at four. Dixie got to the phone first. She called to Hope.

"Your sister's on the line. Maybe you'd better take this in the office."

Damn, damn, damn. Knew it was too good to be true. Lord forgive me, but now what? Hope closed the office door behind her and grabbed the portable phone. She pressed the speaker button.

"Hello?" she asked, not knowing if it was Grace or Faith on the line.

"Hope, it's Faith. I've got to go home. Right away. That stupid, stupid, stupid Beauregard just called me."

Go home? Oh, shoot. "Okay, honey, calm down, please. I can barely understand you. Take a deep breath. Something's happened to the boys?"

"Yes. I can't calm down. I'm so mad I want to kill that man. Isiah got trampled when he fell off his horse at the rodeo. He's got a compound fracture and they're taking him into surgery right now. I've got to go home."

Hope expelled a long breath, her heart sinking to around her knees. "Of course, you do. If he needs care, maybe you can bring him back here to stay with us and we can all help you. Make the arrangements and then let me know when you need to leave. I'll get you to Jacksonville."

"Hope, I'm not coming back. I can't do this. I can't leave my kids and worry about how their idiot of a father will take care of them. He just can't be trusted. I'm sorry, I know I'm supposed to stay, but I just can't."

Faith's sobs tore at Hope's heart. "Listen, let's just take this one step at a time, okay? You take care of Isiah and assess the situation. It makes more sense to decide our future when you know what you're dealing with, right?"

"I'm deciding my future. And the future of my sons. They have to come first and I'm telling you, I'm not coming back. I'm taking them home, and then I'm going to see if I can't get sole custody so they won't be at the mercy of that moron. Tell Eddie to do what he has to, but I'm out of here. Today."

The line clicked and Hope knew that Faith had hung up on her. Her sister had every right to want to be with her sons and Hope had no right to expect her to stay on in Merciful. But then Hope hadn't made the conditions, their father had.

She stared at the phone for another minute. One thing at a time. She had a customer waiting. Color the hair. Wash the hair. Dry the hair. Collect payment.

Then drive Faith to Jacksonville where she would fly off into the setting sun.

Literally.

Hope dialed Eddie's cell phone half-hoping that he wouldn't answer. But he did.

"I just put Faith on the eight-fifteen to Dallas. Lord, I hope Isiah's okay."

Eddie's voice was steady, low. "Boys break bones all the time. I'm sure he'll be fine. And so will Faith."

"I couldn't bring myself to say much. I was terrified to put any more worry or guilt on her shoulders. She only had one small suitcase with her, though. Maybe she will come back."

"Don't worry about it, Hope. Everything will be okay. Where are you?"

"I got off of I-10 about fifteen minutes ago. I'm heading south on 301. Sign says . . . " She strained to see the small letters. "I'm just north of Starke, five miles."

"Okay, you've still got an hour home. Hey, guess what I had to do today?"

Hope groaned. Last thing she needed right now was guessing games. "No idea."

"Had to take one of my clients to Marion County to file a restraining order on her husband."

"That doesn't sound like a lot of fun. Isn't it depressing to have to do things like that?"

"Sometimes." He cleared his throat. "Today was pretty funny, though. He didn't hit her or threaten her or anything."

"Then what was the restraining order about?"

"He blew up the outhouse. She's furious that he wrecked her bathroom."

Erupting with unexpected laughter, Hope slowed down. Even a moment's inattention could mean disaster on this road. Running into a deer or a bear in the road and wrecking her car on top of everything else would be just too much. She did her best to stifle the giggles still rumbling through her. "Not to mention what an unhealthy mess he made. Why did he do it?"

"Said she spent more time in the bathroom than the bedroom and he was sick of it."

"Good grief. Did you get the restraint?"

"Nope. Judge said since the husband had built it for her, he was entitled to take it down, too. He got a fine for illegal use of the M80, though."

"Is she in any danger though? He must have been mad as hell that she got him fined."

"I took her to her mother's place. She said she's not going back until he rebuilds her bathroom, complete with the mirrors and the soaking tub."

Hope shrugged the tension off her back and pressed down on the accelerator again. "Tops my day. I'm going to let you go. Thanks for keeping me company, Eddie. I appreciate it."

"My pleasure, Hope. See you later."

Eddie got out of his car and stood by the front fender, waiting for her to join him. *She looks like she wants to run in the other direction . . . .*

"Hey, you made good time getting home." He stood with his hands in his front pockets, afraid to make a sudden move.

Hope looked at him. "I did. I didn't know you were coming over here tonight. You should have said something." Purse in hand, she walked to the front door, put the key in the lock and went inside the house.

Eddie followed. "Didn't want to give you the chance to say no. You don't need to be out here alone right now."

She dropped her purse and keys on the table in the hallway. "Think I'll get a drink and sit on the porch a while. It's cooling down now."

Not exactly an invitation. "You go sit down, I'll get us both something. A glass of wine maybe?"

"There's a bottle of red open in the fridge. That will be fine for me. Help yourself to whatever you can find." Hope pushed through the wooden door to the porch.

Eddie pulled out two glasses and located the wine for Hope. He grabbed a Corona for himself. *Must be Grace's choice* . . . .

He joined Hope on the porch, setting her wine on the table closest to where she sat curled up on the rattan couch. He sat at the table, his back to the wall where he could look toward the reserve and listened to the frogs and cicadas creak and croak.

"I don't need saving, you know," she said softly as she picked up her wine.

"I know."

"Then why are you here? I mean, really."

"Told you. Every time you're here alone, something catastrophic happens. With a possible murder charge hanging over your head, alone isn't a good thing."

"Any news on Betty Jo's autopsy yet? I checked on the reverend and his condition hasn't changed any."

"Jack would have called you if he had any news in the Betty Jo case. And when I checked the hospital earlier today, they said Shawn's vital signs were stabilizing. The head trauma seems to be reducing. They put in a drain yesterday to pull the fluid off his brain. He could regain consciousness any time now."

Hope put down her glass and held her head in her hands. "I'm glad to hear that, at least. I hope he can tell us what in the world is going on. I didn't think he and Betty Jo had any dealings with each other, so I can't imagine why they would both end up at Orange Lake."

Eddie took a long pull on the cold beer. "Probably better not to guess right now. And, it could have just been coincidence."

"Lord knows I'd be okay with that, but I don't think so."

They sat in silence a long while before Eddie got up to go back into the kitchen. When he returned with another beer, he sat down on the couch next to Hope. He ignored her involuntary flinch.

"You know, when your father walked through my office door, I thought, hell, maybe I'll get a chance to redeem myself with this family. Your father was willing to give me a chance, Hope. How about you?"

He picked the label off the bottle while he waited for her reply. *I know how to wait someone out . . . .*

"I don't know, Eddie. It's not as much about forgiveness as it is about faith. And I'm not sure I have enough faith in my own judgment, to let you get too close."

He put down the Corona and reached for her hand. Lifting it to his lips, he gently kissed her palm. She gasped at his touch, but didn't pull away.

"Nothing wrong with your judgment, Hope. Mine was faulty, not yours."

He leaned toward her, holding her gaze with his. She sat still as a suspicious doe, hazel eyes wide, the tip of her tongue captured in her teeth. He fought to keep his breathing regular, but he was sure she could hear his heart pounding against his chest. *I don't deserve a second chance, but Lord, how I want one.*

"I'll always love you," he whispered, just before his lips touched hers.

Chapter Fourteen

Amnesia

Hope splashed cold water on her face. She'd slept badly after she'd gone to bed. *How could I have let him kiss me?*

Who was she kidding? She'd wanted him to kiss her. She'd been praying that he'd kiss her. And when he had, the sweetest kiss she could ever remember, she'd just about run from his arms and hidden under her bed.

Eddie was showered, dressed and had the coffee on when she walked into the kitchen. A quick look in his direction revealed that he didn't look as though he'd slept much better than she had.

"That couch isn't very good for sleeping on, is it? I should have told you to take Faith's bed." Hope poured them each a glass of orange juice, careful not to look at him as she pushed it his way across the kitchen counter.

"Couch is fine. I can't stand guard and sleep, too."

"Thank you for standing guard. Did I hear your phone ringing a while ago? Is everything okay?"

Eddie nodded. "The hospital called to say that Shawn was conscious. Not speaking or moving well, but conscious."

"We're going to drive to Shands, then?"

"We are. You better let the gals in the shop know that you won't be around."

"Lord have mercy, you're right. Let me call them and fill them in." She disappeared onto the back porch, cell phone in one hand, coffee mug in the other.

"Erma? It's Hope." She gave her friend the information and promised to get back to them as soon as she could. Then she called Dixie.

"Dixie, it's Hope. I need you to open the shop today, okay? Reverend Jackson is conscious and we're going to Shands to see if we can help him with anything. Appointments are light, so you should be okay."

She listened for a moment, smiled, then said goodbye. She stuffed the phone in her back pocket and went into the kitchen.

Hope put her coffee down and fluffed her hair with her fingers. She looked at Eddie. "I'm ready. How about you?"

He looked longingly at his coffee. "I guess I am too."

"Are you sure Shawn didn't say anything at all about going to the lake?" Eddie eased the Cadillac onto the roughly paved road that went past the Blessing farm and ended in the Hammock Preserve.

"He didn't say anything to me and according to Margaret Ann, he didn't leave a note or say anything to her either. Erma happened to see him loading his car on Friday evening."

"You're around the church all the time. Was something bothering him? He hasn't mentioned anything at all?"

Hope banged her fist on her purse. "Didn't I just tell you? I don't know anything!"

"Hey, hey. Simmer down, girl," Eddie warned. "Might want to remember this isn't my fault. And if you're mad about that kiss, I'm not sorry."

Hope looked down at her folded hands. "I'm not mad about the kiss. Let's just not discuss it, okay? I didn't mean to snap at you, though. I'm just so damned scared about everything. The drivers, Faith and Isiah, the murder charge, and now Shawn's mishap is just too much."

Eddie nodded. "We're all concerned about Shawn. He hasn't been himself for quite some time. I've tried to pry it out of him, but he clams up."

"Bless his heart, now that you mention it, I think he's been looking a bit thinner lately, too." Hope answered. How had she not considered that before? Something had been bothering Shawn and she was unbelievably slow on the uptake here.

"I thought so too." Eddie glanced at Hope. "He and your dad were tight. Shawn considered him one of his closest friends."

"Shawn was considered a part of our family. Dad's sudden death was shocking for all of us."

Silence prevailed the remainder of the drive to Gainesville. Eddie stared straight ahead at the road, his hands locked on the ten-two position on the wheel. Hope gazed out the passenger window in silent prayer for Shawn Jackson's health.

Eddie pulled into the hospital lot. "Here we are." He turned off the ignition and opened the door.

Hope swung the passenger door open and joined Eddie on the pavement. "Let's go to information and check on his room. He could be out of ICU and into a regular room."

Eddie stopped at the desk. "Reverend Shawn Jackson, please."

He pulled his business card from his wallet and handed it to the clerk.

The clerk glanced at the card. “Room 235, Mr. Highspring.” She pointed down the long corridor. “Follow the signs to the elevator and get off on the second floor.”

“Thanks much, young lady.” Eddie smiled and winked.

Hope seethed. She knew that dimpled smile all too well. And that wink! Good Lord, at his age, still trying to charm the ladies. *Damnit, he still can. And why should I care anyway? Get a grip, woman!*

They arrived at the room. Shawn Jackson sat huddled in the large green corner chair. The nurse was trying to feed him lunch.

“Hello Shawn.” Eddie said.

Shawn looked at Eddie and blinked.

“Nurse, I’m Reverend Jackson’s attorney, Ed Highspring.” He pointed at Hope. “This is a close friend. Could you fill us in on his condition?

She nodded her head toward the hallway. “Step outside.” They followed her into the hallway. “As you know, Mr. Jackson was brought in to us two days ago. He’s been beaten repeatedly about the head and we’re very happy that he’s regained consciousness.”

“What’s his condition? And the prognosis?” Hope asked.

“He seems to be suffering from apraxia from the blow to the back of his head. He isn’t cognizant of his body or his surroundings, though he’s conscious. The injuries to the left side of his head and the base of his cerebellum have left him disoriented and he hasn’t spoken a word since he was brought in. He will probably have short term amnesia as well, at least for a few days or weeks. Some memories should come back, though.”

“Can we take him home?” Hope asked.

"No. I'm sorry, we can't release him in his current state. However, when he's released, there must be someone to stay with him."

"We can cover that. His housekeeper Margaret Ann has already said she would stay at the rectory and take care of him." Hope looked back at Shawn.

The nurse nodded. "Mr. Highspring, we need you to stop at the nurses' station to sign some papers, if you don't mind."

"Sure. I'll take care of that right now." Eddie followed the nurse.

Hope settled into the high-backed reclining chair beside the bed and took Shawn's hand in hers.

"You sure had us worried, Reverend. I hope you caught some good fish while you were on the lake. I know how much you like fresh fish," she said. Maybe if she kept talking, she wouldn't cry.

The reverend didn't acknowledge a single word, but she kept talking. She told him about Faith's son with the broken leg and how great the new window looked in the shop.

Eddie returned in a few minutes carrying a large plastic bag with the hospital logo on it.

"Any change?" he asked.

"Afraid not. He just stares out the window."

'What have you been talking to him about?"

"I've just been babbling. Actually, I told him all my problems over and over again." Hope smiled. "As a matter of fact, the only time he looked away from the window and at me was when I told him about my fight with Betty Jo the other day."

The nurse entered the room accompanied by an Alachua County Sheriff's deputy. "Excuse me, folks." The nurse interrupted. "This deputy would like to ask you a few questions."

Hope stood while Eddie introduced them. “We’re friends of Reverend Jackson’s.” Eddie pointed to Shawn. “He’s in no shape to talk to you.”

The deputy nodded. “You his attorney?”

“Yes.” Eddie handed the deputy another of his apparently endless supply of business cards.

“Well, Mr. Highspring, it looks like there was a heap of trouble at the lake that involved two people from the same town. Somebody gave the reverend a mean beating. He could have drowned or been killed. We’re real interested in finding out what happened to him.”

“We’re interested, too,” Eddie said.

The deputy looked at Hope. “Did you say your name is Hope Blessing?”

“Yes. A close friend of Shawn’s.”

“Are you aware of Betty Jo Clark’s drowning?” he asked.

“Yes. I heard that on the news.”

“I understand from the reports that you and Ms. Clark had quite a public confrontation a few days ago.”

Hope nodded. “We did, at her bank. She pushed my buttons, and I responded.”

“When was the last time you were at the lake?”

“I don’t remember. It’s been at least a year, I guess.”

“Well, you’ve got an attorney on record, so I can’t discuss this with you any further. I can tell you, don’t make any travel plans, though.”

Hope felt sick to her stomach. “Why? There’s dozens of people Betty Jo Clark screwed over who might want harm to come to her.”

The sheriff wrote in his notepad. “And you’re one of those people, Ms. Blessing.”

Eddie placed his hand on Hope’s shoulder. “Hold it, Hope. You have an attorney and you shouldn’t be answering anything."

No one noticed the tears streaming down Shawn Jackson's face.

Eddie carried Shawn's belongings in one hand and held Hope's elbow with the other one. "Let's get to the car and calm down. Then I want to look through this bag."

"I'm surprised the sheriff's office didn't want his stuff. He didn't hit himself in the back of the head, especially not three times, so there's definitely a crime involved here."

He nodded, unlocked the car door, then held it open until she was settled inside. "Here." He thrust the bag at her and quickly closed the door.

Once he was behind the wheel with the doors locked, he asked for Shawn's belongings. "Let's see if we've got any clues in here."

Hope dumped the contents on the floor at her feet. "His wallet." She picked it up and gave it to Eddie. He looked through it, found a ten-dollar bill, a fishing license dated Friday June 15, and a few photos. Recognizing Percy, Eddie showed them to Hope.

"Lord knows, those two were fishing fools when they had the time." She ran her thumb over the faded photo. She looked down at her feet. "Car keys, keys to the church and the house, and maybe a receipt? It's been wet, I can't really tell what it is."

She handed the crumpled piece of paper to Eddie, then took the wallet and keys and put them back into the bag. "Anything of importance?" she asked without looking at him.

"Doesn't appear to be."

Brow raised, she looked at him. "Want me to put it back in here?"

Eddie started the car and shook his head. "I'm sure it's

just trash. We'd better get back to Erma and Margaret Ann. They'll be worried."

They weren't the only ones. Judging by the look on Eddie's face, he was worried, too.

What is he hiding?

Chapter Fifteen

Broken Pieces

Hope looked out the truck window at the Shands-Gainesville hospital campus. Once they were on West Newbury Road they'd be back in Merciful in a half hour. She wasn't ready to go back. Something was up with Eddie. Her sisters still hadn't checked in. And the Reverend was nearly a vegetable. What in the world was she going to tell Margaret Ann that would offer any comfort? She let out a tiny gasp as she battled the black dread in her heart.

Eddie drummed his fingers on the steering wheel, then looked at her. "How about something to eat? I could use a cup of coffee and some lunch. Missed breakfast, remember?"

She nodded. "Mildred's? They've got a fried egg BLT that's incredible."

Eddie laughed. "I'd forgotten about that place. I used to love the club sandwich. Back in the day when cholesterol didn't matter, that is."

"You know, with all this stress, I'll be gaining weight like a corn-fed hog anyway. Might as well just eat something fun sometimes. And, at least the food's organic there. Although there's something almost unholy about organic and bacon in the same sentence."

They drove several blocks and located the restaurant. "Next problem is parking. I'll go uptown and we'll walk back, that okay?"

She nodded. Walking might make her feel better, though she doubted it. "Sure. I can't remember the last time I strolled through Gainesville. I went to school here you know, and I dash up here to Sally's for supplies when I'm short on something for the salon, but I never just come here to eat or relax."

Eddie locked the car and walked by Hope's side. "You probably don't do much relaxing, anyway. Always were on the go. With your shop and church and all, I'm sure you stay pretty busy."

They stopped at the corner of the town park and waited for the light to change. He took Hope's hand and tugged on it. She fought the urge to lean in closer to him. *It feels so good to have someone looking out for me . . . .*

"Are you going to tell me what's bothering you? You've been a bit strange since we left the hospital."

She didn't answer, preferring to keep her fears to herself, but she shivered. Maybe if she didn't voice them they wouldn't come true. They walked the next block in silence as Hope swallowed to settle her roiling stomach.

Eddie opened the front door to Mildred's Big City Food, ushered Hope inside, and asked for a table near the back.

As they waited for a waitress, she looked at him and finally answered his question. "Nothing's wrong. A bit preoccupied, that's all. People I care about have some nasty stuff going on."

"Hmm," Eddie replied. "Seems like some of that nasty stuff is happening to you, too, Hope. I'd like to help if I can."

Hope followed the waitress, aware of Eddie's light touch at her back.

After placing their orders, which included hot coffee, first and foremost, Hope sat with her hands in her lap while Eddie's fiddled with the silverware.

"Are we going to talk about last night?" He stirred a packet of sugar into his coffee with great concentration.

Hope dumped in two packets of sugar and a long splash of cream. "Nothing to really talk about, is there? Obviously, we both wanted to see what that kiss would be like. As they say, been there, done that. Curiosity quenched."

"Ouch." Eddie winced, then looked out the side window. "I'm thinking I want to know all there is to know about you since we left high school. Why no kids? Were you happy as a minister's wife? Do you enjoy being a business-woman?" He hesitated, then looked back at her. "What I'd really like to know is if you'd ever agree to go out with me sometime. On a date, I mean."

Before Hope could reply, the waitress appeared with their lunches on her arm. Assured they had everything they needed to enjoy their meal, she ran off in the opposite direction. *I cannot believe we're having this conversation. Actually, I cannot believe that I'm thinking about what it would be like to jump in his lap and let him kiss me senseless.* She gulped her coffee.

"Are you going to ignore me and make me pay for being a stupid fool almost forty years ago?"

Hope almost choked on her coffee. "No, I'm not ignoring you. I'm processing your questions. Deciding what I want to discuss and what I don't. I'm not sure why Matt and I never had kids, it just never happened. I was busy, I was happy, it didn't really matter all that much to me. I think having to be a mother to my sisters may have been a factor. I wanted time for me and my marriage."

"Did you love him?" Eddie took a bite of his sandwich and chewed. He looked at her.

Hope swallowed the bite she'd been chewing and shrugged. *What, am I on the witness stand?*

"I thought so. He was handsome and persuasive, and you were gone and I needed to move on. And he was a generous-hearted man who did a lot of good things in Merciful. I was proud to be his wife. Until he was found dead in Betty Jo's bed, that is. And we aren't talking about that." She took another bite of her BLT.

"Fair enough. I think running your business agrees with you. Am I right?"

"I enjoy it. I have control over my life with my business. Or at least, I was under that illusion until lately." She picked up her coffee and sipped at it. She looked at Eddie over the rim. "My turn, Perry Mason?"

"Sure."

"Why didn't you get in touch with me when you settled in Ocala? I was thirty before I agreed to marry Matthew, you know. You were already divorced by that time, or so I've been told."

He nodded. "I didn't feel I had any right to walk back into your life. What credible explanation would I have for my leaving with Betty Jo when you were the woman I loved?"

Okay, one question settled. "How do you plan to do that now?"

"I don't. I plan to plead insanity and throw myself on the mercy of your heart."

"Let me see if I've heard you correctly," Hope rushed, feeling a mixture of elation and righteous indignation rise up into her throat. Her cup clattered on the table as she all but slammed it down in front of her. "Are you saying that you still love me? Now? Today? Right here in the middle of all this crap that is making me crazy?"

He put his hands up as though he feared she might lunge across the table at him. "I guess I am, Hope."

They sat staring at each other for a long minute. Then the waitress came by to check on them. When they declined dessert or more coffee, she laid the check on the table and scurried away.

"That's a stupid plan, you know," Hope said as she got to her feet and leaned over to collect her purse off the back of the chair. "You're still a great kisser, though." *I must be insane.*

Eddie scrambled to his feet to follow her as she marched toward the door. "I'm probably better than I was in high school at quite a few things. I'd like a chance for us to get to know each other again as adults. See if there's something still special worth fighting for?"

Hope led the way to the front door of the restaurant. She pulled it open, then glanced over her shoulder. "Let's get through the next few weeks and maybe resolve some of the mysteries around us. Then I'll give it some thought."

"Fair enough," Eddie said. But he lightly held her left elbow as they walked down the street. And Hope didn't pull away.

Eddie pulled his car into the driveway at the rectory. Margaret Ann waved at them from the front door. They joined her in the kitchen, each pulling out a chair and sitting at the wide table.

"So, how's he doing?" She clasped her hands in front of her, her big brown eyes creased with worry.

Hope smiled. They were people of faith, therefore they could believe that Shawn Jackson would be restored to them. Lord help her, if she had to lie to set Margaret Ann's mind at ease, she would just have to do it and apologize later.

"He was very badly beaten around his head, so he's not quite himself, but the injuries are healing and every day he's a little bit better. Maybe he can come home in a few more days, if someone can stay with him, that is. Otherwise, he can stay with us out at the Blessing Farm."

"Oh no, that's fine. I told you I'd just stay here with him. And Erma will help, too. She wants you to call her at the shop when you can."

Eddie looked toward the sink. "Have you found anything out of place in his office by any chance?"

Margaret Ann shook her head. "I dusted and emptied the trash basket. Didn't see anything that looked wrong. His sermon is in the middle of the desk. I didn't touch any of that. Maybe I didn't work homicide, but I learned enough as a cop to leave things be for a while."

"Would you mind if I take a look while I'm here?" Eddie got to his feet, but waited for her answer.

"No sir, you go right ahead. Are you looking for anything special?"

"I don't know what I'm looking for. Just some explanation of what happened, I guess."

"Well, you go right ahead. Hope needs to call her sisters. They both called here this morning. Your cell phone not working?"

Hope pulled her phone from the pocket on her purse. When she flipped it open, it remained dark. "Forgot to charge it, I guess. I used it earlier this morning, then we hit the road and I didn't check it."

Margaret Ann's laugh was hearty and Hope's spirits lifted. *Maybe we'll all be laughing again, soon . . . .*

"I think that man is distracting you. That's a good thing, mind you. You could use a good man to distract you from things."

Or not . . . . "Will it be all right for me to call Grace and Faith from this phone?" Hope asked, pointing to the phone hanging near the kitchen door.

"Sure. I'll go see if your lawyer needs anything. You call your sisters." She disappeared through the doorway. Hope heard her call out to Eddie.

Grace's phone rang a half a dozen times before she answered it. "Grace Blessing. Who's calling?"

"It's me, Hope. Are you all right? Where are you?"

"I'm fine. How the hell are *you*? Been calling you all morning and all I get is your voice mail."

"Phone's dead. I'll charge it when I get home."

"Well, Craig and I dropped off the Tallahassee load without a problem. I picked up our empty trailer, too. And, we might have a lead on the guy causing us all this trouble."

Craig? Hmmm. "That's encouraging, but I don't want you doing anything that will get you hurt. Turn the information over to the sheriff's office and let them handle it." Hope dropped into the chair.

"We still need more information, but we'll be careful. I should be back at the farm by dinner time tonight. Have you talked to Faith today?"

"She was my next call."

"She's much calmer and feeling like an ass. Isiah's surgery was this morning and it went well. He's begging her to let him go back to his father's when he's discharged."

"Oh, and how did she feel about that?"

"Not real generous. She wants Beau drawn and quartered for letting Isiah get hurt. I tried to tell her kids get hurt, but she cut me off."

"Well, they *do* get hurt. Both of you came home with various sprains and broken bones and neither of you rode rodeo. It just happens, no matter how careful you try to be. They aren't babies. Beau can be a jerk, that's true, but he wouldn't hurt his kids."

"I know. If she's calmed down, she might listen to you, but probably you just need to leave it alone another day or so. He's going to be in the hospital until the end of the week. They have to make sure he doesn't get an infection."

The fatigue from worrying about them started to settle into her shoulders. She felt the slump and sighed. "Okay, sounds like great advice. I'll check in with her, then I'll have Eddie drop me off home."

"I heard the good padre is doing better today? Glad to hear it. I was afraid you'd be going back into the preaching business." Grace chuckled.

"He's conscious, but he isn't functioning yet. They're still feeding him on a liquid diet to make sure he can swallow. He didn't know either of us. I'm worried. His injuries are serious."

"I'm sorry to hear that. Do they think he'll make a recovery?"

"The doctors aren't saying anything for certain."

"Well, if God listens to anyone, it's you. I've got to go, Sis. Craig's just pulling into the truck stop where we left his pickup. Don't worry, just pray. Isn't that what you always told us? I'll see you later at home. We'll talk if you need to."

"Thanks," Hope said, though Grace had already ended the call.

She dialed Faith's number and let it ring until the voice mail picked up. *Maybe she's at the hospital . . . .*

"Faith, it's Hope. My phone's dead, but Grace said Isiah did real well today and I'm so glad. I'll be home by five. You're all in my prayers. Call me and fill me in. Love you, honey."

Eddie and Margaret Ann came back into the kitchen together. "I don't see anything that's useful in figuring this all out," Eddie said. "Your sisters okay?"

"They're fine. I'm ready to go home, charge my phone, and take a nap. I'm sure you're about ready to get home, too."

He looked at her a long moment, then smiled like a cat that had just cornered a mouse. "I guess I am, lady. Your chariot awaits."

"I'll let you know if I find anything, Mr. Highspring," said Margaret Ann as they went out the door. He stopped and turned to face her.

"Call me Eddie, please. And I appreciate it, Margaret Ann."

He held the door for Hope as she got into his car. Once on the road, she looked at him. "What was that about?"

His brows were drawn into a frown. "There is some link between Betty Jo and Shawn and I can't figure it out. I just asked Margaret Ann to keep her eyes and ears open for that link, that's all."

"Great. Let's just hope that whoever drowned Betty Jo and smashed Shawn's head in doesn't come by the rectory looking for the same information."

"Actually, I'm hoping they do. After I drop you off, I'm going back there. Margaret Ann is going to leave in a few minutes and go home. I told her to stay away. I'll go back to the rectory until we get this figured out. Staying too close to you is a serious threat to my self-control."

Chapter Sixteen

Picking up the Pieces

Hope awakened to whistling and the smell of fresh brewed coffee permeating her room. She rubbed her eyes, stretched and rolled out of bed. She went down to the kitchen and found Grace packing a cooler.

"Why, good morning, sleepy head," Grace said.

"Sleepy head? It's six-thirty. I don't need to be up at this time. What the devil is going on here, Grace?"

"I'm doing a run today."

Hope yawned and scratched her head. "What kind of run? I thought we were caught up."

"Well, since we agreed we'd double up and Manny and Patrick aren't back until later this morning from that Alabama run, I'm doing a Fort Meyers run with Craig."

"Craig? Craig Mattheson?"

"Yes, Hope. Craig Mattheson."

"Weren't you driving with him yesterday? And are you sure he isn't the guy who tried to sabotage us? Do we need any more trouble than we already have?"

Grace placed her hand on her sister's shoulder. "Sis, I thought we straightened all of that out. Craig didn't steal accounts from us. It was Betty Jo that did it. He wants to make it up to us and he offered to help out. I think he's one of the good guys."

Hope waved her hand around the kitchen. "So that's what all this is about."

"Yep. I thought I'd pack us lunch so we didn't have to waste time at a restaurant. We can just pull over to a rest stop."

Hope smiled. "Sounds like it could be a bit cozy, too."

Grace blushed. "Speaking of cozy, I found a man's comb in the bathroom this morning. Anything *you* want to tell me?" A horn beeped in the driveway. "That must be Craig now. You can tell me about the comb later. Now you've got time to make up a good story. See you late tonight, Sis." Grace headed to the kitchen door. "Any word on when Faith's coming back?"

"I haven't heard from her. I'm not all that sure she's coming back at all. I'll call her today and see if I can find out what's going on. Keep your eyes and mind on the road, young lady."

Hope helped herself to the remaining coffee and took a sweet roll from the breadbox. "Nothing beats an early start to your day," she muttered.

Hope unlocked the salon early since she was already awake anyway. As she turned on the coffee pot, she thought about Grace. She seemed so cheerful.

Could she have a crush on Mattheson? Hope couldn't argue with how Grace's Army-take-charge attitude had helped salvage the trucking company. If Mattheson had shown some interest in Grace, Hope was happy for her, but she still felt he couldn't be trusted. *Grace isn't very experienced in matters of the heart and I will personally kill that man if he hurts my little sister . . . .*

She busied herself getting the salon set for business. Erma came through the door. "Hi Hope. You're an early bird this morning."

"Grace had to leave early today, so I thought I might as well come in. I may leave after Dixie gets here, though. There's a lot of book work at the shop that needs to be done."

Erma sat down. "So let's have it, Hope. What happened to Shawn?"

Hope filled Erma in on Shawn's condition. "So that's all we know so far. The hospital will keep Eddie posted on any changes and we'll bring him home as soon as we can."

"I can't figure out why anyone would want to hurt the reverend." Erma shook her head. "He's such a good man. Always there to help others out. Does the Lord's work. Can't understand it." She headed for the door. "I've got to run and open up the dress shop. Talk to you later, honey."

Eddie spent the morning in Gainesville at the main branch of the Alachua County Library searching through pre-1980 newspaper articles from Atlanta, Georgia. He looked away from the screen, rubbed his eyes, and stretched.

He looked down at the smudged and wrinkled newspaper article in front of him that read, "Child Killed by Three Teens." *Why would a copy of this article be with Shawn's belongings at the hospital?*

He continued reading the archived article. He scrolled down the screen and stopped. "Hot damn! There it is."

The library director approached him. "Sir, you must be quiet. This is a library, you know."

"Sorry about that, ma'am. I found the information I needed. Thank you." He grabbed the copies from the printer, stuffed everything into his briefcase and nearly ran out the door.

Hopping into his car, he touched the auto dial on the rearview mirror for Hope's number.

When she didn't answer her phone, he left a message. "It's Eddie. Just wanted to tell you I will be in Atlanta for two days. I phoned the hospital to let them know they can call you as the contact for Shawn until I get back. Take care of yourself."

Grace glanced in the rear-view mirrors as the rig ate up the miles on the Interstate. She sure had a lot going on. As an engineer, she had no trouble keeping things on track, and as an Army officer, she excelled at getting the best out of her soldiers. But as a woman, she was having some mighty issues.

"Hungry, Grace?" Craig asked, breaking into her reverie.

She nodded. "Sure am, actually."

Craig nodded toward the right. "Pull over at the next stop. It's right up ahead."

Grace put the right blinker on, slowed down, pulled off the highway to the rest area, and parked.

"There are some picnic tables down further. Let's stretch out a bit."

Craig grabbed the cooler while Grace lifted out the basket and they headed down the hill to the picnic tables. She pulled out a red tablecloth, napkins and utensils from the basket. Then she opened the cooler and placed drinks and sandwiches on the table. *I sure hope I'm not making a fool out of myself. Really, a tablecloth? Jeesh.*

"This is a mighty fine spread. Has to be the first time I've ever eaten food from an authentic picnic basket." Craig's eyebrows rose as she flipped the tablecloth over the food stains from earlier, less tidy picnickers.

Grace felt her face get warm. "It's all Hope had at the house, figured it would do."

Craig chewed his sandwich. "I wasn't complaining, Grace. It's fun and it was very thoughtful, so thank you. You handle that rig pretty good for a girl. Where did you learn that?"

She shrugged. "I've been around trucks my whole life. I grew up with the trucking company, and in the Army, if it has wheels on it, you need to know how to move it."

"Fort Myers is a mighty tight town for trucks. Those streets were made for bicycles. You did good, girl." Craig continued eating and drinking. "If you're tired, I can drive the rest of the way."

Grace pushed her chips around with her index finger, hating the heat she could feel in her face–and the rest of her body. She cleared her throat. "That would be great. And thanks for riding with me. Two pair of eyes are always better than one."

"Not a problem."

Grace looked at him, feeling on safer ground. "How do you think we can catch the guy that's hassling us?"

"I've got a couple of ideas. I'm thinking it's one of two guys in my company, but since they usually have each other's back, we're gonna have to try and split them up. Let me think on it some more and I'll let you know what I come up with. Okay?"

"Just don't take too long to figure it out."

Craig collected their trash and placed it in the can. "Hey Grace, do you like movies?"

"Sure. Haven't been to one in a while though. I couldn't even tell you what's playing these days."

"There's a new suspense film out, I'd like to see. I was wondering if you would join me, say next Friday night?"

Grace felt the blush rush from her toes to her nose. She busied herself tying her boot which didn't need tying. "Sure," she mumbled.

They climbed back into the rig and pulled away, smiling—Craig at the wheel.

Hope worked on the Amazing Grace books until five o'clock. The small air conditioner struggled to keep the eight-five-degree temperatures out of the office, but the metal building had no insulation and the heat was winning. It was probably approaching one hundred degrees in the garage.

The company was moving in the right direction. They'd be able to escrow enough money to make several consolidated payments if the court ordered them to do that next week. Hope smiled. A month ago, she'd thought everything was lost. Now, thanks to her sisters, Eddie, Patrick and Manny, they had a chance.

She shut down the computer and dialed Faith's cell phone number. Faith answered on the second ring.

"Hi, Sis!" Faith nearly shouted.

"How are you and how is my nephew doing?" Hope pulled a can of ice tea from the office refrigerator and held it to her forehead.

"He's doing just fine, even if he did scare ten years off my life. The hospital is going to release him tomorrow and he wants to go back to Beau's."

Hope sighed. "You going to let him go?"

"No, but I've agreed to leave the boys at their grandparents' house. They'll be safe there."

"So why are they okay with Edna and Russ and not Beau?" Hope asked.

"I charged to Beau's place like a mother bear protecting her cubs during hunting season. I read him and his brainless twit of a wife the riot act."

"Good for you."

"I told them since the boys are still minors, I would haul both their butts into court, charge them with neglect and child endangerment, and strip Beau of his visiting rights. And, he would still have to support them."

"Good going, Sis."

"Thanks." Faith cleared her throat. "I was kind of wired. When I calmed down a bit we compromised. The boys get to stay at the ranch under their grandparents' supervision, and Beau can visit any time he wants till I get back."

"Great. Edna and Russ seemed like decent folks the few times I met them," Hope said.

"They really are. I've kept a cordial relationship with them. It's their son who's a waste of a human being."

The Saints Go Marching In chimed from Hope's cell phone. She lifted it off the charger on the desk. "Oh it looks like a

Gainesville exchange, I better take it," she said to Faith. "Can you hold on for me? This is probably the hospital."

"Sure, I'll wait," Faith said.

Hope hit the hold button on the desk phone and picked up her cell. "Yes. This is Hope Blessing." She listened to the caller. "He has? That's great news. Mr. Highspring is out of town for a few days but I'll let him know. Thank you."

She took Faith's call off hold. "What's going on?" Faith asked.

"Shawn's talking, which means he's improving. I have to call and let Eddie know." Hope took a deep breath. "How do you feel about coming back?"

Faith's sigh was long and tired. "The boys will be fine and I'd like to be there with you and Grace when we get to tell the bank to pound their note where the sun doesn't shine. I'll check into a flight back and let you know. Maybe I can be home by tomorrow afternoon. If not, I'll be back as soon as I can."

"That is great! You let me know and we'll come get you at the airport. Talk to you later."

Home. She sounds happy to be coming back. Daddy, maybe you weren't so crazy after all.

Hope finished off the iced tea and dialed Eddie's number. When he answered, she put him on speaker. "Hi Eddie, great news! Faith's son is going to be fine and she's coming back as soon as she can get a flight. And the hospital just called. Shawn is talking."

"Well that is real good news. Glad to hear that Faith is coming back, too. Any idea what Shawn's talking about?"

"No, they didn't tell me about the exact conversation, just that he seems to be regaining some of his motor skills and he asked for you, today."

"I'll be back tomorrow. I've gotten about all the information I can from up here. Did they say when he could be released?"

"No, only that you should call them. Maybe we can have him home in time for Tuesday Bible study. Seeing all his friends again would probably be good for him," Hope said.

Eddie was quiet. "I'll call them and get the details. I'm sure he'll need all the support he can muster from his friends. Don't forget to lock the doors and I'll see you tomorrow."

"Sure. Tomorrow." Hope ended the call and put her cell phone in her pocket. *What, or who, was so all-fired important in Atlanta?*

Chapter Seventeen

Trust

Sunday morning dawned clear and bright. Hope stretched and tossed back the sheet, planting her feet firmly on the floor. She'd slept better than she had in days. When she pulled back the curtains, overnight rain had left the grass and plants glistening in the sunlight.

Grace had come in around nine and they'd watched an old Boris Karloff movie together, sharing popcorn and Jack Daniels. As kids, they'd always loved those blasted mummy movies, despite the bad dreams they'd had later.

Grace only mentioned that the trip to Fort Meyers had been uneventful and that Craig was working on a plan to catch the saboteur. Hope wondered what Grace wasn't saying about the time she'd spent with Mr. Craig Mattheson. But since her sister never was a person to say more than she absolutely had to, Hope didn't bother prying any further, opting to enjoy a quiet evening at home instead.

She padded across the hallway to brush her teeth. Three toothbrushes stuck up out of the cup on the small countertop.

She smiled. Here they were, aging peas in a pod and she was delighted. *I never realized how much I missed them. How will I let them go again?*

She glanced at her reflection in the mirror. It would be ten times harder, now. Now she loved them as an adult sibling, not as a frustrated older sister. Her life had gotten colorless without them. *I won't be happy with colorless anymore . . . .*

"Hey sis, you gonna be done any time soon?" Grace hollered through the closed door.

"In a minute." As promised, she hurriedly finished brushing her teeth, ran a comb through her tangled hair, then yanked open the door.

"Thanks," mumbled Grace, pushing past her. The door shut and Hope smiled.

Grace had never been a morning person. It was amazing that after all the years in the Army, she hadn't changed all that much. Sure, she was tougher on the outside, and she spoke goals in terms of twenty-four hours, but she still wasn't much for morning conversation.

Their mother had always hopped out of bed with a smile that never left her face, or so it had seemed. She'd always be in the kitchen waiting for them when they clamored down the stairs in the morning. Something hot and yummy would be waiting for them, as though Sarah Blessing had made it her personal mission in life to bring smiles to her daughter's faces every day. Hope smiled at the memory of the aromas of cinnamon, bacon or peaches in the house.

Hope had all she could do to make the coffee. A minister from Gainesville was going to be doing the service for them today and she couldn't be late to Bible study, but she wouldn't take another step without a cup of coffee. She sat on the stool at the kitchen counter and rested her chin in her hand.

Grace pushed through the door and sat beside her. "You going to church?"

"Yup. Wanna come along?"

"No, but thanks. I want to go over the trucks, do some maintenance. Manny's coming in this morning and I want to make sure we're ready to go next week."

Hope looked at her sister. "I did the bookkeeping yesterday. We're doing okay, and I don't know how to thank you for all your help. And for who you are around here."

Getting to her feet to pull down two mugs from the cabinet, Grace shrugged. "Daddy didn't give us a lot of choice, did he? Besides, it's been kind of fun."

"Well, thank you anyway. You could have said 'no way' and gone back to the Army, but you didn't. I'd have loved you even if you didn't stay, you know."

"I know." Grace pushed the mug across the counter at Hope, then placed the container of half and half alongside the mug. "Have some coffee."

"Have you decided about the Army yet? Are you going to stay in or try something else?"

"I'm leaning toward getting out. If I put in my papers by the end of the month, I can take my full retirement starting in September. Not sure if I'll settle in New Mexico or come back this way. Still working out that part of things."

Hope fought to keep from wrapping her arms around her sister, an act she knew Grace would hate. "Well, you know you're welcome here for a while or forever. It's up to you."

The clock in the hallway chimed eight times. "That's zero-eight-hundred hours. If you're going to make church on time, you'd better hop to it." Grace sipped at her steaming coffee.

"Yes, Ma'am," Hope said, hopping off the stool with a sharp salute. "You be careful in the garage while I'm gone. I don't like you being here alone."

Grace grinned. "I own a Glock and know how to use it. I'm never alone."

Margaret Ann, Erma, and several of the regular women of the Merciful Evangelical Church were waiting at the door when

Hope arrived. By the looks on their faces, something was wrong.

"Why do you all look so upset?"

Erma sighed. "The visiting minister isn't here yet. What are we going to do?"

"We'll do Bible study like we always do. If he's not here when we're ready for service, we'll think of something. It isn't a Communion Sunday, so it's not so bad."

Margaret Ann's face relaxed. "We could do a reading, tell everyone about the Reverend, do a prayer service for him, then just let everyone go home."

"We sure could. God tells us to come together, He doesn't dictate what we have to do after that, except to look out for one another." Hope smiled at them all. "We do that, right?"

Everyone nodded. Bibles tucked under their arms, purses hanging from the other, the foursome marched into the Fellowship Hall, which had been rearranged into a study center.

The area closest to the kitchen was home to three six-foot tables and would accommodate a dozen adults. Coffee was already perking in the large party pots and the aroma filled the room.

To the left and right near the doorway were tables arranged in a horseshoe fashion for the children. Ages three to nine were on the left side, ages ten to sixteen were on the right. Colorful partitions had been moved into place to provide some separation for the groups. Joseph's coat of many colors was depicted on the side of the wall of the area for the youngest kids. She and Matthew had spent days painting those panels and had more paint on each other than on the screens. Hope smiled. *A lot of good memories in that marriage, too.*

Margaret Ann and two helpers had poured paper cups of juice for the children and put two trays on each of the tables. The clock above the entry door said nine-thirty. Hope turned on the ceiling fans, and moved around the room closing the curtains against the warm morning sunlight.

On cue, the doors opened and families entered the hall, each with their Bibles in hand. *This is what makes church fun.* Hope went to the counter at the kitchen window and poured herself a cup of coffee, then took a seat at the table. No matter what happened today, life was good. Shawn was getting better, Grace was happy with life, Isiah would be fine, and Faith was coming back home.

She didn't need a minister to lead her in prayers of supplication or thanksgiving. She'd become a praying fool in the last three weeks. *And He's heard them all.*

Eddie's car was parked at the rectory when church let out. Hope, Margaret Ann, and Erma had thanked the visiting minister for helping in Shawn's absence and sent him on his way. A soft-spoken, pleasant man in his eighties, Hope was sure he was going straight home to take a nap.

The women entered the rectory through the side door that led into the kitchen and found Eddie at the table. Before Hope could ask them to stay, Erma and Margaret Ann whisked themselves out the side door with conspiratorial winks at each other and Eddie.

"You look tired," Hope said, trying to ignore the fact that Eddie had winked back.

"Hit a lot of traffic coming home. A truck overturned on the Interstate which slowed things down considerably."

Even knowing that their trucks weren't on the road didn't stop Hope's heart from skipping a beat. "Well, Grace is out at the house working in the garage. Lord knows I don't know much to help her, but I'd best get home and see if she needs anything. We'll be having ham for dinner if you'd like to join us, probably around four. Faith won't be back until tomorrow, I think."

"I'd like that." Eddie looked at his feet, then gazed at Hope. "I know you're champing at the bit to ask me what I was doing in Atlanta, but I can't. Client privilege."

"Jeesh, you know, I'd just about forgotten that you have more clients than the Blessings. I wouldn't want you to jeopardize your legal obligations. It just would have been nice if you'd said, 'Hope, I have to go to Atlanta for a client and I'll be back when I can.' But you just disappeared with that flaky phone call."

"I'm sorry. I'll try to communicate better next time. Forgiven?"

"If you went to Atlanta for anyone other than Shawn Jackson, you are."

He swiped a hand across his eyes and she had her answer. "That's what I thought." She moved to the door and stopped with her hand on the knob. She didn't turn back to look at Eddie.

"I sure don't know what's going on around here and I don't like it. I guess I'm angry because he's my friend and I'm going to be the last one to know what he's done that he needs protecting from."

As she pulled open the door, a thunderous shudder shook the building. The old wooden-framed windows rattled and the doorknob shook under her hand. "What the heck?"

Eddie bolted toward her. "Sonic boom, I hope. The Air Force and Navy don't consider the Sabbath a day off." He looked at her. "Hope . . . ."

Before he could say another word, the sound of sirens filled the air. "So much for a quiet Sunday afternoon," she said, then walked through the door.

As Hope drove toward Magnolia Road, fire trucks raced past her. Her heart quickened. She pulled over and dialed Grace's cell phone which went straight into voice mail.

"Oh Lord, no . . . . " Pulling back onto the road and keeping pace with the emergency and rescue vehicles, it only took another mile before Hope knew either the farm or the preserve was on fire. Didn't much matter since the outcome could be the same.

Thick black, oily smoke filled the air, making it almost impossible to see anything to the west of the house. The house looked intact but for some broken windows. But the garages, where Grace had spent the morning working on the trucks, were fully engulfed in terrifying, tree-top licking flames.

God, please, no. Where is she? She can't be in there! She cannot be in that building! Hope skidded her pickup to a halt on the road, a hundred feet from the property. The Fire Marshall wouldn't let her pass.

"I'm sorry ma'am, but you need to stay back where you're safe."

"You don't understand. My sister is in that building. You've got to get her out of there."

"Stay right here." He walked a few feet away from her and spoke into his shoulder mike.

When he returned his face was gray. "Are you sure she was inside the building? Any chance she wasn't there?"

Tears blurred Hope's vision and clogged her throat. "That's where she was when I left for church. She was checking the trucks. We've been having some problems, and..."

His hands held her shoulders, but she struggled against his grasp. "Calm down, please. Does she have a cell phone?"

Hope gulped air and nodded. "I called her, but it went to voice mail. If the black SUV is in the yard, she's home." Her face brightened. "Maybe she's in the house?"

"What's left of the SUV is in the driveway by the big bays. If she's in the house, she didn't answer the door. Would she be too frightened to answer the door?"

She shook her head. "She's career Army Corps of Engineers, sharpshooter. Not much scares Grace. But she could be stunned or hurt, maybe outside the building?"

He stepped away to talk into the mike again. Hope saw firefighters run around the garage perimeter, then toward the house, circling it twice. The Marshall returned to her side. "No one outside the buildings."

No, God, no. Please God, no, not Grace. Not my sister, Lord. I'll do anything, just please save Grace...

She stared as though she was watching a massive movie screen and the main prop looked just like their home. The fire crackled so hot the tops of the magnolia trees were wilted and brown, leaves raining down everywhere. Hunks of smoking, steaming metal were strewn all over the front lawn, forming crater-like indentations. The stench of burning diesel fuel filled the air. She sank to the ground on her knees and clutched her hands against her pounding chest.

Eddie found Hope sitting in the pickup truck when he arrived twenty minutes later, her Bible clutched to her chest, her tears still wet on her cheeks.

"I thought you were going to Ocala for a couple of hours," she said staring out the windshield.

"I was. Got almost to the interstate before I realized that boom sounded a lot like an explosion." Without another word, he slipped into the passenger seat, put his hand on her shoulder and together they watched the firemen pour heavy streams of foam on the garage.

Two hours later, the firefighters had the fire out. Two twisted, metal heaps sat awkwardly beside what had been the garages.

The bad news was that the fire had burned so hot, they might not find any remains until they could sift through the ashes of what had been the Amazing Grace Trucking Company.

The good news was they hadn't found Grace's body.

Chapter Eighteen

Up In Smoke

Shattered glass covered the office in the Blessing's farmhouse. Eddie shoveled it into mounds he could pick up and put into heavy-duty trash bags as Hope sat on the sofa, clutching her cell phone.

"Do you have work gloves around?"

Hope got to her feet. "Why we most surely did," she drawled. Hope pointed out the hole in the wall that was once a window. "They're right out there in the truck garage." She tiptoed around the mountain of shattered glass and peeked out. "Oh, but guess what? It's not there anymore." She burst into tears. "It blew up!"

Eddie dropped the broom and cradled her in his arms. "I'm sorry Hope. I'm so sorry for . . . for everything," Eddie whispered.

She sniffed and raised her head. "This isn't your fault. I just keep thinking about Grace and what if she's out there, somehow?" The sobbing started all over again.

"What the hell happened?" shouted Grace as she stormed

into the room with Manny on her heels.

Hope freed herself from Eddie's arms. "Grace, you're okay!" Hope hugged and kissed her sister. "I thought you were dead!"

Grace pointed to Manny who stood beside her, his mouth partially open. "Manny and I drove out to Big Bob's Diesel Parts out on Highway 206. We needed a part for one of the trucks. We called all the local places, but no one was open on Sunday." She walked over to the desk. "I left a note for you," she said shuffling papers around.

"With that kind of blast the note must have been blown off the desk. It's probably buried under the glass," Manny said.

Grace looked around. "Well as long as you guys are all right, it doesn't matter where the damn note is."

"Hey Manny," Eddie said. "Do you have your pickup here?"

"Yeah. What do you need?" Manny asked.

Eddie picked up the broom and rested it against the wall. "Let's go out to the Home Depot and get some plywood. Can you give me hand boarding up these windows?"

'Sure, let's go." Manny took his keys from his pocket and the two men left.

Grace grabbed the broom and started sweeping. "What the hell happened, anyway? Everything's gone?"

"We don't know what happened except that apparently when one truck exploded, it ignited the other one. When the diesel fuel went up, so did the building. So, we're down two trucks, the office, the garages and all our maintenance equipment. But the good news is, we're insured because I got that all paid up last week. We can rebuild the garage. Thank the Lord I use the bank system for the accounting and records, so I can get to that tomorrow. Most of our client files are in here. Let's move the file cabinet and the desk contents into the dining room as soon as we get this cleaned up."

"How about trucks?" Grace asked.

"The two that were fueled are gone. The two that need repairs are still out there, but damaged. That's a major setback for us."

"Maybe I can help out with that," Grace offered.

The two sisters worked on removing the broken glass from the office, and moved the files, filing cabinet, and important papers into a corner of the dining room.

Reassured that the records were secure, Hope told Grace how she'd come home after church to find everything going up in flames, including Grace's rental car.

Grace turned a bit pale. "Manny and I left around twelve-thirty. If the place exploded less than a half-hour later, maybe someone was watching the place. Didn't want to kill anyone, just scare us silly."

"Could be, and that makes this even creepier. Someone is sitting in the woods watching us run our lives?"

"I agree. Very creepy. Tomorrow I teach you how to shoot."

Hope shuddered. "Not me. I don't think I could kill *anything*, let alone a human being. It would be a waste of ammunition."

"Sis, if someone broke in here and tried to kill me, would you do whatever you could to protect me?"

"Of course."

"That's all I'm talking about. Trust me, the mama bear in you will give you true aim, for sure."

They both lifted their heads when they heard the tires of a vehicle crunch on the driveway. Grace glanced through the window.

"They're back. Go see if we can't put something together for dinner. I've got a call to make."

Eddie and Manny began toting lumber, power drills and boxes of screws to the house. "Coming through," Manny yelled. They set up the wide sheets of plywood and began to board up the window openings.

Grace ran upstairs to her bedroom, pulled her cell phone from her purse, and dialed Craig's number. "Hi Craig. It's Grace."

"Hey, Grace, how are you doing?"

"Not too well here today. There was an explosion in our truck garage. We lost the garage and two of our trucks. In plain words, somebody blew us up, Craig."

The long silence on Craig's end puzzled Grace. "Craig, are you there?"

Craig cleared his throat. "Grace, I'm really sorry to hear that. Is there anything I can do to help?"

"Oh, I don't know. You wouldn't have an extra rig lying around, would you?"

"As a matter of fact, I do. I'll be glad to lend you a truck. When do you need it?"

"I'll call you tomorrow and let you know. Thanks, Craig. I gotta go."

She placed her phone on the nightstand, laid across the bed, and placed her hands on her chest. Craig's reaction, or rather, non-reaction bothered her. He sure didn't sound surprised. *Maybe Hope is right. Maybe he is the saboteur. But why?*

I thought his feelings for me were real. I guess I'm just damned naive when it comes to men. Or, at least men and romance. Shaking off her disappointment, Grace dialed Faith's number.

"Hi, Grace. What's new?"

"Well, let's see. We no longer have a truck garage."

"Why? What happened?"

"There was an explosion. We lost two trucks and the

garages, too."

"My God. Is everyone all right?"

"No one was injured. But we're pretty shook up around here."

"How's Hope doing?"

"She's devastated, of course, but she's doing that strong thing she does. She's trying to have a positive attitude about it. She thinks the insurance money will be enough to rebuild. I hope she's right. She's really upset at Eddie about something, but he's still here working his ass off to board up the house. How is Isiah? Are you planning on coming back here?"

"He's coming along. They're settled in at the ranch with Beau's parents. I can't get a flight out until Tuesday, so I booked that. I'll arrive on the 4:02 flight. Couldn't let you two have all the glory, you know."

Grace chuckled. "That's good. You can help us rebuild once again. Hope and I can pick you up. We'll see you then. Safe journey."

Grace put her phone in her jeans pocket and went downstairs and joined the threesome in the office. Manny and Eddie had just finished putting the last of the screws into the top of the final board. They began straightening up the room.

Hope finished running the shop vac over the floor. "Well, there you are. Where did you go?"

"I went upstairs to call Faith. I filled her in on what happened today and asked when she's coming back."

"Did she know?" Hope asked.

"Tuesday afternoon. She was pretty upset about the explosion. She was just glad no one was hurt."

"Maybe it won't look so bad by Tuesday," Hope said. "Eddie phoned in our claim to the insurance company answering service already. They said an adjuster will be here first thing in the morning."

Grace hugged her sister. "We've come so far salvaging this company. This explosion might be a setback, but we'll get through this too. Who knows, could be a blessing in disguise."

"We'll just put this in the Lord's hands. He always provides." Hope returned her sister's hug.

The Saints Go Marching In chimed from Hope's phone. "Hear that, Grace? That's a sign. The saints *are* looking out for us." She answered her phone. "Hello?"

She listened. "Shawn!" she screeched. "How are you? It's wonderful to hear your voice." She hit the speaker button and laid the phone on the desk.

"I've been trying to reach Eddie, but he doesn't answer."

Hope noticed Shawn's slurred speech was slow but steady. "Eddie's been out of town on business, but he got back this afternoon."

"Do you know where he is?"

Hope looked at Eddie. He shook his head and left the room.

Hope frowned and wondered what that was about. "He's helping Manny fix something out in the yard. How are you feeling?"

"I'm much better. The doctor said I can go home tomorrow. Can someone come and pick me up?"

Manny left before dinner and promised to be at the farm in the morning. Grace, Hope and Eddie pillaged the refrigerator and cleaned it out, eating the leftovers right out of their containers. Hope was so tired she ached everywhere.

"I sure hope I had enough insurance on that rental car," Grace moaned. She leaned back in her chair and pushed her plate to the side. "I can't remember what the hell I took on it and the paperwork was in the glove box."

Eddie laughed. "Yeah, we put *all* our important papers in the glove compartment, never thinking someone is going to blow up our car."

"Not funny." Hope stood and began gathering the containers off the table. "I'm just so thankful that whoever blew up the trucks waited until Grace and Manny were gone. I don't give a damn about anything else."

Edie nodded. "Hey, I saw Mr. Clark this afternoon when Manny and I went to Home Depot. Maybe he'll be more receptive to recasting those loan notes than his daughter was. I always thought he was a good man."

Hope frowned. *Is he crazy?* "Gee, I can see that conversation. 'Excuse me, Mr. Clark, but even though I'm a person of interest in your daughter's disappearance, would you redo my loans and give me a workable rate?'"

Grace snorted. "Now *that's* funny. Look, this isn't the time to even think about that stuff. Let's get cleaned up here and get to bed. We've got a lot of work tomorrow and it's all going to require a lot of focus." She collected the food boxes and dropped them into the sink in the kitchen.

Hope opened the dishwasher and began to fill it with what was left on the counter. Eddie looked at Grace. "Why don't you go up to bed? I'll help Hope finish here and then we'll all call it a day."

"You've got a deal. If you're staying the night, why not sleep in Faith's bed? That couch sucks."

"No, I'll take the couch. I want to be able to hear if someone tries to get into the house."

"In case you didn't notice, there's a cop outside. He'll be there until they finish the investigation. Whoever set that explosion today is long gone." She wished them goodnight and headed up the stairs.

"Grace is right." Hope put the soap in the dispenser cup and locked the dishwasher door. "Faith's bed would be far more comfortable."

He shooed her out of the kitchen and switched off the light. "*Your* bed would be far more comfortable, and that's why I'm sleeping on the couch."

Chapter Nineteen

Staying Alive

"Okay, everyone quiet down." Grace stood in the doorway to the kitchen and by the look on her face, Hope knew her sister was in no mood to listen to any sass.

Manny and Patrick stood side by side near the door to the back porch with large paper cups of Quiki-Mart coffee. A clear plastic drop cloth covered the rattan couch where Eddie and Hope sat. Everything was soot-covered.

"Since Hope's getting to be an expert on insurance claims, she'll talk with the insurance company today about the trucks and the building. Obviously," she waved toward the dark unidentifiable masses out near the skeletal remains of the garages with her free hand, "they are a total loss. The good news about that is that the insurance should pay off the loan on the one, and the old Mack can be replaced with something newer. We hope."

Hope's stomach was calmer, but she felt as though something inside her was about to snap. "Dad's insurance policy provided for leasing replacements in the event a truck is lost in an accident or stolen," she contributed. "So when I get done with the insurance company, I'll get on the phone with that outfit in Ocala and see if I can't lease us two trucks so we can make our deliveries this week."

Manny piped up. "Me, Patrick, and Miss Grace will go down and pick them up. We can leave in an hour and by the time you've made arrangements we'll be ready to start back. But maybe we shouldn't bring them here."

Eddie snorted. "With all the investigators around, this is probably the safest place in Florida to park them."

"We need to get the broken windows on the house replaced today, and you," Grace pointed at Eddie, "will need to go pick up Reverend Jackson and get him transported home. Margaret Ann will be waiting for you this afternoon."

"Hello? Anybody home?" called a male voice from the front of the house. Grace disappeared, and the voice was silenced. A moment later she reappeared.

"Craig? What are you doing here?" Hope got to her feet, trying to decide if she should invite him to join the pow-wow or send him on his way with a flea in his ear. *Is he friend or foe?* She still wasn't sure.

"I want to help. I know Grace thinks I might have had something to do with this, but I'm telling you I didn't. I called every man into the office this morning and we had a come-to-Jesus meeting."

Hope gestured for Craig to join them, hoping she wasn't inviting the fox into the henhouse.

"Find out anything useful?" Grace asked.

"Word around my place is that Mike Reiner may be the guy we want. Several of my boys saw him talking to Betty Jo more than once in the past few months. He and his buddy Richie didn't show up for the meeting, even though I talked to them about it last night."

Grace squared off in front of him. "That doesn't necessarily let you off the hook, Mattheson. If you were smart, you wouldn't want to be seen talking to the person who bankrolled you just to bankrupt us." Hope felt like she was a tennis match, her gaze bouncing from Craig to her sister and back.

His face reddened as he faced Grace, but he didn't flinch under her glare. "I'm done defending myself. If you need a couple of trucks until you can get this straightened out, you can have the rigs Mike and Rich drive. As of today, they're off my payroll."

Eddie shot a glance at Hope, then looked back at Craig. "That's a generous offer, Craig. Everyone's really on edge right now and nobody knows who they can or can't trust. It isn't personal. I hope you understand."

"Sure I understand, but I don't like it. It *feels* personal. That bitch set me up just like she set you all up, the only difference is that I knew her well enough to protect myself the second time around."

Hope's chest unwound a bit as she reached her decision. She stood and held out her hand. "Craig, we're going to Ocala for those trucks, but there *is* something you can do if you really want to help."

He shook her hand, then cocked his head to the side and looked at her through narrowed eyes. "What do you need?"

"Rehire those drivers. Keep them busy and keep tabs on them. I think we're going to have to catch them in the act if we're going to stop this insanity. If you cut them loose, we won't know where they are or what they're up to."

"Lady, in case you've forgotten, Grace could have been in that fire yesterday. These boys ain't playing around. I think the Sheriff should pick them up and talk to them," Craig reminded her.

Hope's stomach did a flip and she swallowed. "Craig, I will never, ever forget that Grace could have died yesterday. I have no idea if I'll ever recover from those heart-stopping hours that I thought she was gone. But that's why we've got to force those snakes into the open. The Sheriff can't hold them without evidence and they may or may not be scared off. Might make them more determined."

"I'm not sure how you're going to protect yourselves until we get them corralled, but I'll go find them and rehire them if you think it'll help."

"I do. Tell them we've met and that you think you've got me on the ropes now that all our equipment is gone. Tell them our drivers won't work for you and you need them back. See what kind of reaction you get. Then we'll figure out how to get them to make a move and we'll shut them down."

"Well, I'm not paying them to hurt anybody. I run a good outfit. And those boys were with me before Betty Jo cleaned me out. I thought I could trust 'em. Guess I was wrong."

"When it comes to Betty Jo, a lot of people found out they figured wrong," Eddie said to no one in particular.

Craig looked at him. "Sounds like you knew her yourself."

"He was husband number one," Hope pointed out. "But even if Betty Jo was behind the other incidents, why blow up our trucks? There's nothing to gain if the goose laying the golden eggs has died."

Craig shook his head. "No idea. This whole thing is weird, but it pisses me off that I'm being accused of this stuff. That's not my style. I might punch a man in the eye if he deserved it, but I don't go sneaking around behind his back."

Hope laughed, feeling just a little lighter now that they had some kind of plan. "Good to know, Craig. Look, I've got tons to get done and you all need to get out of here and get busy with your part of the plan. I want a check-in call from each of you, every two hours."

Everyone nodded, then they filed out through the house, single file.

Now, to face the insurance company . . . .

It was a little before three p.m. when Hope pulled into the driveway at the rectory. Eddie's car was there. She stepped out of her car, locked it, took a deep breath, exhaled slowly and walked to the door. She knocked and went inside.

"Hope, it's sure good to see you." Margaret Ann motioned with her head toward the living room, so Hope moved in that direction.

"Good to see you, too. Is the reverend getting settled in?"

"Sure is. He's doing just fine. He and Eddie are playing a game of checkers."

Hope smiled at her friend. "That's wonderful. I just stopped by to say hello and welcome him home. I won't stay too long."

"You stay as long as you like. I'm making a pie, so I'll be in the kitchen." Margaret Ann turned and vanished along the hallway.

When Hope entered the small parlor with its floor to ceiling windows, she was warmed to see Shawn looking better than he had since her father had passed. *Maybe it's memories that age us, not life itself.*

She cleared her throat and the men looked up. "Hope, thank you for stopping by," Shawn said with frown of concern. Eddie was telling me that you've had a busy few days. I'm so sorry to hear about the fire at the farm."

She shot a look at Eddie, who shrugged. "Yes, well, no one was hurt and I think we'll be able to replace what we need. Tell me how you're feeling."

She tossed her purse on the sofa and dropped onto the ottoman near the checkerboard. "I hope you're beating him," Hope said to Shawn as she pointed at Eddie.

"No, I'm afraid he's beating me. But the doctor said to play one or two games a day to get the brain working again. I'm just glad he didn't suggest chess. I was never much of a chess player to begin with. I hope I'll regain my checkerboard acumen in time."

"I'm sure you will. You know I'm going to pick up Faith at the airport tomorrow. She's a very good checker player. I'll make sure she stops by daily just to keep you on your toes."

He laughed softly, wincing as he did. His long fingertips rubbed at the side of his head.

Hope didn't miss the gesture. "Maybe you should lie down for a while. Don't overdo things just because you're home. We want you healthy, so just take it slow, okay?"

"Yes, I'll take it slow. Everyone's been so kind. I don't want to be a burden any longer than I must. I wanted to ask you, do you know why I was at the lake by any chance?"

"I'm sorry, I don't. Erma mentioned that you put your fishing gear in the car, so I guess you were just going to try your hand at landing a few bass. Wasn't Shawn's fishing license in his wallet, Eddie?"

He studied the board. "Sure was. We don't know why you were attacked, Shawn, but the Sheriff's working on it."

"Too bad I can't help with this, but I can't remember anything except having dinner that Friday night. Hope, tell me, is Betty Jo finally working with you about those loans?"

She looked at Eddie. His eyes reflected as much surprise as Hope felt. *What do I tell him? And what did Shawn know about the loans?*

"No, she isn't. Betty Jo's dead. Some sort of accident at the lake, they think."

She watched the healthy color drain from his face and tears fill his eyes. "Oh my, that's a terrible thing. We just talked last Thursday about you two working things out. I was so hoping my talk had helped."

He struggled to his feet, clutched the table, then grasped for the back of his chair. "My head is hurting too much. I'm going to lie down for a little while, if you'll forgive me."

He stretched out on the sofa and Hope pulled the homemade quilt over him. "You just go ahead and rest. Margaret Ann and Eddie will be here if you need anything. I've got to stop by the shop before I head home."

Eddie walked Hope to the door. "He didn't mention Betty Jo until he saw you. Do you think he's remembering actually talking to Betty Jo or is he remembering something he thinks that he did?"

"No idea. Still can't tell me what you discovered in Atlanta, right? Since you have more information than I do, I'm sure you'll figure it out. I do know that Shawn's not capable of murder. He didn't kill Betty Jo."

Eddie held the door open for her. "I wish I was as sure as you are."

In the quiet of the shop, Hope put on the coffee and grabbed her supply list. As happy as she was that Shawn was home and looking so much better than he had in the hospital, she was still terrified that nothing had been done about Betty Jo's death. Every time she thought of herself as a murder suspect, she almost threw up. She knew that her innocence was no guarantee that she wouldn't do jail time, no matter what her attorney said. What would happen to her family then? *The farm? The shop? Her clients?*

She stopped and took a sip of coffee. *Get a grip.* Her imagination had her convicted and wearing institutional jumpsuits. *I don't look good in orange.* She let out a nervous laugh and shook her head. *Enough.*

She replaced the shampoos and towels in the front of the shop and wrote up her supply list. Then she took a look around. She was as ready to open tomorrow as she'd ever be.

For the time being, she'd run the trucking company and her salon from the office in the back, she just didn't want anyone to know about it.

She rinsed out her cup, turned off the light and locked the door. When she turned to walk off the porch, she bumped into the chest of a tall young man, probably in his late thirties. "I'm so sorry. Can I help you?"

He looked at her as though she hadn't spoken. "I was lookin' for a haircut."

"We're not open on Mondays. We'll be here tomorrow morning, though. Why not come back and we'll take care of you then?" The hair on the back of her neck stood on end. She attempted to step around him.

He didn't move. "I'm not sure I'll be around here tomorrow." He looked at her steadily, then shrugged. "If I am, I'll stop by."

He stepped off the wooden sidewalk and began to stride down the street. "Wait!" she called. He stopped and looked back.

"What's your name?" she asked, wondering which of the two men he was.

"Mike. See ya."

Hope started to shake. She clutched the arm of the wooden rocker and lowered herself into it. Erma came out a moment later.

"Lordy, you look like you've seen the devil himself. Can I get you something?"

Unable to speak, Hope trembled in the chair. After several deep breaths, she whispered to her friend, "Call the Sheriff's office for me, will you?"

As Shawn slept, Eddie stood looking out the window toward Main Street. When he saw the Alachua County Sheriff's car pull up in front of Erma's shop, his heart nearly stopped. Now what?

He dialed Hope's cell phone number, but it went to her voice mail. He raced into the kitchen.

"Margaret Ann, what's Erma's number at the shop?"

"Speed dial number three, right there." She pointed to the phone on the kitchen wall.

He called the shop and counted the rings. *Come on, come on, come on . . . .*

Erma answered on number five.

"This is Eddie. Is Hope all right?"

Erma spoke softly as though she didn't want to be overheard, so he had to strain to hear. And to keep from screaming at her.

"What did he say? Why was she frightened enough to call the Sheriff?"

Again, he listened. His shoulders slumped. "Yes, I'll ask her about it when she gets home. Just let her know that I called, would you please?"

He hung up the phone. He was juggling way too much emotion these days on far too little sleep. He didn't know what in the world he'd do if anything happened to Hope now. And he didn't know how he could help the client sleeping in the next room. If he kept Shawn's secret, was he putting Hope in jeopardy?

Percy, what in the world have you gotten me into?

Chapter Twenty

Mixed Blessings

Hope was in the hair salon at eight o'clock, doors locked and looking over her shoulder at every sound. She truly hoped that the man named Mike with the nasty vibes would not come back for his haircut—ever.

The smell of fresh brewed coffee lightened her spirits. She missed Margaret Ann's company and help, but knew it was more important for Shawn to have round-the-clock care, than Hope to have her shampoo girl. It would only be for a week or two—or so they all hoped.

She glanced at the Jimmy Buffet "Five O'clock Somewhere" clock on the wall and laughed out loud. Leave it to the hippest island-dweller in the country to recognize the marketability of an idea that made people smile twenty-four hours a day. She had ten minutes to her first appointment. Time for another cup of coffee.

She fixed a cup and went into the office to relax for a few minutes. Her appointment calendar wasn't jammed full, but without Margaret Ann, and Dixie off on Tuesdays and

Wednesdays, Hope was spread a bit thin today. She sighed. *Will all this ever be over?* She was the kind of tired that sort of settled in your bones like a fog on the marsh.

Faith's return to Merciful had been quiet. The twins had walked through the door a little after seven last night. Hope had dinner ready and waiting and before ten, they were all fast asleep with their new windows locked, their new alarm activated, and Grace's Glock loaded.

Well, I wonder what today will yield. She finished her coffee, went to the sink and rinsed out the mug, and walked to the door to unlock it and swing her OPEN sign around. The bell over the door jingled, and Hope looked up.

"Mrs. Hutchin, how are you today?" She lowered the chair and swung it toward the older woman.

"I'm doing just fine, thank you. A bit of arthritis in my left hip that's been bothering me, but I can't complain. I heard a terrible explosion happened at your house Sunday! Lord have mercy, we felt it all the way out by the Ice House. I'm glad that no one was hurt."

Since she was the sister of the Alachua County Fire Marshall, who obviously spoke with the Marion County Fire Marshall, Hope wasn't surprised at her knowledge.

"Yes ma'am, we were very fortunate. Nothing damaged that can't be replaced."

"Well you girls have certainly had more than your share of bad luck the past month or so. I do hope that things will settle down for you."

Hope decided not to point out that luck, good or bad, had nothing to do with the chaos in their lives. She didn't have the energy to have a conversation with anyone, about anything. "Thank you," she replied.

When the cut was done, Hope got out the hand-held blow dryer and a curling brush. In less than ten minutes, she was applying the customary hair lacquer that provided hold and shine. Mrs. Hutchin's silver hair looked stylish and impenetrable.

She rang up the sale and took the money. When Mrs. Hutchin gave her a five-dollar bill for a tip, Hope thanked her with a hug. "See you next month!"

Hope used the dryer to blow the hair off the chair onto the floor, and then swept the hair into a pile in the corner. Before the day was out, she'd sweep a mountain of hair off the floor.

Her nine-forty-five appointment was late, so she dashed into the bathroom, washed up and combed her own hair, then grabbed a bottle of water from the refrigerator in the office. She heard the bell ring and hurried to the front of the salon.

The tall, uniformed deputy that had warned her not to leave town ten days ago was standing in the doorway. Hope's breath caught in her throat at the same time her stomach turned over. She squared her shoulders and put on a smile.

"Deputy. What can I do for you today?" *As if I didn't know this was coming . . . .*

"Miss Blessing, you're going to need to come with me to the office. We have some questions that need answering, now that we've confirmed Ms. Clark's death is a homicide."

Hope leaned against the back of a stylist chair and sighed. *Oh, my God.* "I'm sorry to hear that, Deputy. Of course, I'll come with you, but can I call my sister to cover the shop for me? With all the losses we're taking, I just can't afford to send my customers somewhere else. I'm sure she can be here in ten or fifteen minutes."

"Yes ma'am, that's fine. You can call your attorney, too if you'd like. I'll just wait here, and we'll go to Gainesville together." He moved to the back of the salon near the bathrooms and coffee station and sat in a chair by the wall. He was only steps from the back door, so he could see that Hope couldn't leave her office and get by him.

The phone rang before Hope could get to her desk, so she answered the portable at the appointment desk. "Faithfully Yours Salon."

She listened and smiled. "Well, Agatha, I'm going to have to leave the salon for a bit, but Dixie and Faith will be here, so you come in around two and we'll get you done then, how's that?"

She listened again, thanked the caller, and hung up the phone. She looked at the deputy. "That was my nine-forty-five, so there's time to get my replacements in. Give me a few minutes."

Hope went into her office and called Dixie who promised to be there by ten-thirty. Then she called Faith.

"Sis, you need to come down and cover the shop for me. I have to go to the Alachua County Sheriff's offices. There's a deputy here now."

She nodded while she listened to Faith's outburst. "Yes, call Jack Edwards and ask him if he can meet us at the station, if not, just let him know that's where I'll be. But I need you to get here as soon as you can. Dixie will be here in about forty-five minutes and we have an appointment due at ten-thirty. You do a good wash, give her a coffee and Dixie will be here."

Again, she listened. "Gotta go, Sis. You take care and I'll call you as soon as I can, okay?" She clicked off the call, shrugged out of her smock, hung it on the back of the office door, and picked up her purse.

She closed the office door, turned off the coffee, checked the lock on the back door and swung the CLOSED sign to face out. "I'm ready to go if you are." When the deputy was out of the salon, Hope locked the door, then went into Erma's shop.

Erma was standing just inside the door, wringing her hands. "Are you okay?" she asked softly.

"I'll be fine if I'm not sick over all this stress. Listen, I can't talk, but Faith is going to come open up the shop in a few minutes. Here's the key. Dixie will be here, too. I'll call you later."

Without waiting for any confirmation from Erma, Hope dashed out the door and met the deputy at his car. He held open the back door. Hope closed her eyes. "What, no cuffs?"

He smiled, but since his eyes were hidden behind his aviator sunglasses, she wasn't reassured. "You're just coming in to answer some questions for us, ma'am. You aren't under arrest."

"I know, I was only teasing. Needed some humor, you know? Not every day that the entire town watches me escorted from my place of business to a squad car and then driven off in the back seat." *It's a damned good thing that Daddy's not around to see this.* She swallowed the urge to cry. She was doing far too much of that these days.

"No ma'am, it probably isn't an everyday occurrence. Watch your head, ma'am."

With Hope safely inside the inescapable back seat, the deputy got into the car, called in to his dispatcher and then buckled his seat belt. Hope clicked hers, too. Then she turned to face the window and closed her eyes.

Lord, please help me with this. I'm so scared I've got pains in my chest, but I know I don't have anything to hide. Give me courage and grace, Lord. And watch over my family, please. Amen.

"You okay, Mrs. Kane?" the deputy asked once they were on the road to Gainesville.

"I'm fine, thank you. And I don't go by the name Kane anymore. My name's Blessing."

"Yes ma'am. We'll be at the office in about twenty minutes. Doesn't take so long with the college kids gone for the summer."

"I can imagine Gainesville must be insane when the Gators are playing at the Swamp, right?"

The deputy chuckled. "Yes ma'am, we're all on duty when they play the home games. Gainesville PD, the Sheriff's department and the Florida Highway Patrol."

Hope put her head back against the seat and closed her eyes. She focused on taking deep breaths and relaxing. She felt a calm and peace that had been missing in the past few days.

Next thing she knew, the deputy was calling to her. She'd fallen asleep. *Oh, great. With my luck, sleeping on the way to interrogation is a sign of guilt.*

With a slight grip on her elbow, the deputy escorted her into the station. He nodded at an officer behind the glass just inside the doorway and a buzzer sounded. He opened the door and led her through into a hallway of office spaces, not unlike those at the power and light company.

After several stops and turns, he sat her in a room that had a table and four chairs, a water cooler, a television mounted to the wall and a bench bolted to the wall. Unlike the television shows, there was no glass or mirrored wall. *Probably video cameras, these days . . . .*

"Detective St. Clair is on a call, but she'll be with you in a few minutes."

"Can you see if there's any word from Jack Edwards, my attorney?"

He nodded and withdrew from the room, closing the door behind him. Since Hope's purse had been locked up in a locker outside the room as part of the standard protocol for "visitors," all she had was her bottle of water. She opened it, took a drink, and deliberately twisted the cap back on. With steady fingertips, she traced the letters on the label, focusing on barely touching the label itself.

Well, here I am, America's most wanted hairdresser. She swallowed a laugh. *Even dead, Betty Jo is causing me grief. I wonder what God is trying to teach me in all this . . . .*

Before she could continue her musings, a dark-skinned woman with the loveliest cheekbones Hope had ever seen walked into the room. Her jet-black hair was plaited and hanging over the front of her left shoulder. Her badge hung on the belt of her khaki slacks and her short-sleeved blouse was a pale green.

She extended her hand. "Ms. Blessing? I'm Detective St. Clair. Are you comfortable? Can I get you anything?"

Hope noticed the handshake was firm and cool, but not the kind that screams, "I'm in control here, so don't forget it." She relaxed a bit.

"I'm as comfortable as I can be under the circumstances, Detective. I have my water. I don't need anything else. Can you tell me if Jack Edwards has called or come in yet?"

The Detective went to the wall phone, repeated the inquiry, listened a moment, then nodded. She hung up the phone and sat down at the table. "He's called to say he's on his way. Should be here in a few minutes. He'd rather you didn't answer any questions until he arrives."

"Thank you. I'm an intelligent woman, Detective, even if I've never been inside a police station before. I won't answer anything I don't like, how's that? When Jack gets here, you can ask those questions again if you need to."

St. Clair smiled. "That works for me. The first thing I'd like to know is why you thought you needed an attorney. And one of the best criminal attorneys in the region, besides."

"I didn't think I needed one, but my father's attorney, Eddie Highspring, thought I should be prepared to defend myself if I was charged with anything in connection with Betty Jo Clark."

"Well, we aren't charging you with anything, we just want to talk." Someone knocked on the door and she got up to answer it, opening it to permit a man to enter.

"Hope, I'm sorry to keep you waiting but your call was unexpected. I was in the middle of a deposition." As though they'd known each other their entire lives, Jack Edwards sat down next to her and gave her a kiss on the cheek. "We'll have you back to Merciful in no time."

She smiled at him. He was fifty-ish, a bit over six-foot, sported light blue eyes and shaved his head to a polished shine. His tie was missing, his shirt sleeves were rolled up and his navy-blue slacks had a razor-sharp crease. He nodded at the detective to begin.

She looked at her notes. "Ms. Blessing, how long did you

know the deceased?"

Nonchalantly Jack nodded at her. "Since I was about ten, I guess. That's when Betty Jo's father bought the bank and the mansion, and they moved into town. So, that would be forty-six years."

"You had her arrested for breaking and entering your home a few weeks ago, is that correct?"

Hope frowned. "Not exactly. After my father died a few weeks back, I was staying there. Someone broke into the house. I called 911 and the dispatcher told me to get out of the house. The deputies came out of the house with Betty Jo in handcuffs. I didn't have much to do with it. I didn't know who was in the house, only that they were not supposed to be there and they were tearing up the office."

"What was she looking for?"

"I have no idea. We didn't discuss it. My sister Faith thinks she was looking for the mortgage note."

Jack put his hand on Hope's arm and leaned close to warn in a voice the detective couldn't hear. "Don't volunteer information, Hope. Just answer the questions in as few words as possible."

Hope looked at him. She was sure her annoyance showed on her face, but he just winked at her and smiled. She sighed.

"Your lawyer probably won't let you answer this one, but I have to ask it anyway. Why does your sister think Ms. Clark was looking for the mortgage note?"

"Don't answer that." Jack's tone was gentle, but his blue eyes were hard as a stormy sea.

"Why not?" Detective St. Clair looked at Jack, her face revealing nothing.

These two would be great poker players, that's for sure. Battle of the Titans, anyone?

"Because she's hired me to advise her and that's my advice. Her reply would be conjecture, anyway."

"We're just talking here, Mr. Edwards. But I'll bring in

her sister and ask her myself. Or, do you represent the entire family?"

"No, you'll leave my sister out of this. For heaven's sake, it's no secret since the day I told Betty Jo off at the bank. She refused to work with my father regarding the mortgage on the homestead, my business building, or the trucks. She had begun foreclosure proceedings."

Jack's sigh was long and deep. "She wouldn't have hauled your sister in here. She's bluffing. You're your own worst enemy. Why did you want me here if you're not going to listen to me?"

Tears began to build in Hope's eyes. She opened her bottle of water and took a long swallow, then capped it again. "Because Eddie told me that if I was asked to come in to answer questions, I had to let you know. So, I did. But I haven't done anything wrong, and neither have my sisters. I see no harm in telling the truth." She squared her shoulders and looked at the detective.

St. Clair fought a smile that she couldn't keep from her eyes, while Jack just shook his head.

"You have no idea how many people are sitting in prison right now that have said those exact same words," he said.

Hope felt the color drain out of her face. "I'm sorry, Jack. I don't belong here and I'm doing the best I can."

"I know, Hope. Just listen to me, please." He patted her hand, then sat back watching the detective.

"Ms. Blessing," St. Clair started, "let's talk about that day at the bank. I have the witness statements right here." She turned the folder so that Hope could see neatly typed forms on the Sheriff's department letterhead. Hope blinked but said nothing.

"You have a question?" Jack asked.

"Ms. Blessing threatened Betty Jo in front of a dozen witnesses, just about a week ago. Three days later, the woman goes missing, and two days after that, her body is fished out of

Orange Lake. She was drowned, Ms. Blessing, after someone tried to strangle her."

Hope placed her hands on the table. "That is horrible. But I didn't do it."

St. Clair shrugged. "Fair enough. We're about done. All you need to do is tell me where you were on Saturday the nineteenth and you can go home."

"Let me think a minute. My sister Grace had to take a truck to Alabama, so she left mid afternoon. My sister Faith and I were home, at the farm. Why?"

"The coroner has determined that she died on Saturday, between six and ten p.m."

Hope looked at Jack. She had an alibi, but she wondered if Shawn did.

"I'm sorry Detective, as I've said several times, I did not kill Betty Jo."

"We're looking at all three of you, you know. I'll be talking to your sisters, too."

Jack got to his feet. "You can talk to anyone you want. The women had nothing to do with this." He motioned to Hope. "Let's get your purse and get you home. We've just pulled the plug on this interview."

St. Clair looked sad, her dark eyes fixed on Hope's. "I'm sure I'll be seeing you again, real soon."

Chapter Twenty-One

Suspects

Faith pulled up in front of Faithfully Yours Salon and parked her rental car. She jumped the two steps from the street to the covered boardwalk and rushed through the door of Erma's shop, nearly out of breath.

"What in the world is going on?" she asked the dressmaker. "Did you talk with Hope before she left?"

Erma shook her head. "More like she talked to me. Left me the key, said you'd be by for it. Then she skittered out the door like she was on the way to a lynching. Her own. And got ushered into the back seat of a police car looking pretty darned scared."

"Oh, no. I should just close the damned shop and go see what's going on, but she'd kill me." Faith shook her head and squared her shoulders. "Okay, I'd better get things going over there if she's got appointments coming. I hope she remembers the only thing I know how to do is shampoo and sweep floors."

"She said Dixie is on her way, too. You'll be fine. If you need anything, just let me know. I'll leave the door open. If you prop open the salon door, I'll be able to hear you if you call out."

Faith took the key and walked to Hope's shop. After unlocking the door and propping it open with a large brick, apparently kept in the corner for just that reason, she turned on the lights, tossed her purse and the keys into Hope's office, then dumped the coffee out and started a new pot. *She hasn't been gone long, this is still almost hot.*

By the time the coffee was brewed and Faith had swept up the hair left in the pile from the first customer, Dixie was whistling her way through the door.

"Hey, kid! How ya'll doin'?"

Faith tucked the broom in the small closet near the bathroom. "I'm fine. You must be Dixie? I'm Hope's sister . . . . "

"You're little Faith. I'd know you anywhere. Your sister has your pictures all over her office wall. You a beautician?"

"Nope, more like I can make coffee, answer the phones, and scrub heads. You wouldn't want me cutting anything you cared about."

Dixie laughed. "Well, then we'll be just fine. I'm gonna look over the appointments, then we'll figure out what we have to do. Is Hope okay?"

Faith looked at the floor. *How much does Dixie know? What's safe to tell?* "I'm not real sure. Seems the Sheriff came by and took her to the office. For some reason, they want to pin this Betty Jo thing on Hope."

"Hell, honey, they just want to close it, may not matter who's really guilty. But don't you worry, she'll be fine, bless her heart." Dixie moved to the appointment desk and opened the book. "Okay, this will be easy enough. Good thing the last one is at two, because I've got to pick up my grandkids at daycare today. I didn't get a chance to tell Hope I had to leave early."

"You don't look old enough for grandkids, Dixie. Listen, if she's not back by then, you just go, and I'll close up."

"Well, you're a darlin'. I just turned fifty last month, but it's only a number, right? That coffee smells great. Let me get a cup and then I'll be ready to go."

At ten-thirty a woman and her daughter walked through the door. Dixie put the daughter in her styling chair. The mother promised to be back in a half an hour. Faith watched in awe as Dixie chatted and cut simultaneously, non-stop. The teenager laughed and turned pink in the face when Dixie fussed over her large green eyes.

"You'll be fighting off the boys with a stick, honey. You just wait and see," Dixie said as she used the curling iron to finish the last wave near the girl's ear.

"I don't think so, but it's nice of you to say. I do love my haircut, though. Thanks, Miss Dixie."

Her mother came back, paid the bill, and whisked her daughter away. The next client was ten minutes late, but the fourth one was five minutes early.

Dixie had consulted an index card from the butterfly-covered box that Hope kept on the work-station, then mixed the color for Mrs. Buchanan.

She applied the hair dye to the gray strands. "You have a gentle touch, dearie," the old woman said.

"Thanks." Dixie continued brushing the formula onto her head. "I'm only leaving the color in for fifteen minutes. Then Faith will give you a good rinse and conditioning."

"Fifteen minutes? Why so short? I don't want this gray stuff showing. I want my honey-blonde color back."

Dixie smiled. "I know, Mrs. B, but hair thins out as we get older. Gray hair is especially delicate."

"Okay, it sounds like you know what you're doing. Fifteen minutes it is."

Dixie put the dye bowl and brush in the wash-up sink and motioned to Faith.

Feeling like a fish out of water, Faith jumped to attention when Dixie pointed at the coffee pot. Faith poured Mrs. Buchanan a cup of coffee and handed her a weekly celebrity gossip magazine. "Here you are. I'll set the timer and be back in fifteen minutes." She felt like she was going to crawl out of her skin. *When are these people going to get out of here? I need to find out if Hope is okay . . . .*

Dixie was shampooing her next haircut. Faith swept the hair cuttings from the floor around the chairs, and threw a load of towels into the washer. The hair color timer rang.

The bell above the door announced another customer. The gentleman walked up to the desk. Dixie was putting the finishing touches to her client's new blow out.

"Can I help you, sir?" she asked, turning just far enough to look at him.

"Yeah. I want a haircut. Do I need an appointment?"

"You don't need an appointment today. Only on weekends. I'll be with you shortly. Pour yourself some coffee, and have a seat." Dixie pointed with her rat-tail comb to the coffee area and resumed blow drying.

Faith settled Mrs. Buchanan into Hope's styling chair, and removed the towel from her head. "Time to blow dry and curl and you'll be on your way."

Dixie finished her client's hair and rang her up. "Thanks, JoEllen. Same time next week?" She entered the appointment in the book for three o'clock the following Wednesday.

Dixie swept the hair from the floor beneath her styling chair. She walked over to Faith and whispered, "I'll give this guy his haircut, but you'll have to collect and clean up. I have to be out of here in twenty-five minutes."

"No problem. I'll handle it. I'll get him shampooed and ready while you finish Mrs. B." Faith nodded toward Hope's styling chair. "I'll turn the sign around and lock the door, so we don't get any more walk-ins. I need to get out of here, myself."

Dixie nodded and busied herself getting done. Faith went to the register to collect from Mrs. Buchanan. "Do you like it?" she asked the older woman.

"Very much. I like it a lot." She turned to Dixie and handed her a five-dollar tip. "Thank you, Dixie. I'll see you in a few weeks."

Dixie gave the woman a hug and turned back to the young man in her chair. "I'm sorry to rush you around like this, but we're closing early today." She combed and clipped, noticing that he didn't need as much of a cut as a style. "You from around here?"

He shook his head. "I had business over this way for a few days. I'll be heading back when I'm done this afternoon. Want to look good for my trip home."

Dixie finished trimming his dark sideburns, then handed him the mirror. "I squared off the back a bit, hope you like it."

He looked and nodded. "It's fine, thanks."

After blowing the hair away from his collar with the hand-held dryer and dusting his neck with some talcum powder, Dixie apologized again.

"I'm sorry to cut and run, but my grandkids are waiting for me. Faith will take your money and see you out."

Dixie dashed into the office, picked up her purse and blew Faith a kiss as she vanished out the back door of the business.

"That'll be ten dollars," Faith said, waiting at the register for him to pay.

"Say, you're one of those Blessing sisters, aren't you?" His sneer made her uneasy.

"How did you know that?

"You ladies are popular these days. Everyone is talking about the Blessings." He glanced at the front door.

She heard a click, then saw a flash. In his left hand was a switchblade knife. The blade must have been a foot long.

"Please don't do this. I've got kids," Faith pleaded. "Why are you doing this?"

"I've got to teach you Blessing sisters a lesson. One by one if I have to."

She could taste coffee in her throat, bile right behind it. *Oh my God, please make him leave.* A sob escaped. She clasped her hand over her mouth.

"Good, you're scared, aren't you?"

When she didn't answer, he lunged at her, stuck his face in hers, the knife against her upper arm. "Beg me, Blessing. Maybe I'll reconsider."

"Yes, I'm scared! I'm terrified! And I don't understand. Why us? We don't even know you," she cried.

"But I know you," he screamed, his face white with rage.

Faith jumped, her heart beating like a rapid-fire rifle. This time she choked the sob back and grasped for words. Words that would keep him from killing her. Keep her from leaving her sons without their mother. Hope and Grace without their sister.

"Listen, this is ridiculous. The haircut's on the house. Just go out the front door and we'll forget all about it."

His face turned beet red. "Sit down and shut up, you bitch." He threw a can of hairspray at the mirror which shattered into pieces.

Faith screamed and huddled in the nearest chair, her face covered with her hands.

"Where's your sister?"

She looked at him, tears unchecked running down her cheeks. "My sister? Which one?" She hated how much fear showed in her voice. She took a deep breath and swallowed. This had to be Mike, the man Hope told her about.

He began to pace. "You don't know what you did, do you?"

Faith shook her head in silence. Tears started again as the realization hit her. *I'm never gonna see my boys again . . . .*

Mike settled himself against her at the chair. He pressed the knife point to her throat. She felt the warm trickle of her own blood.

"You're responsible for my dream girl's death. My Betty Jo."

That stopped the tears. Faith wrinkled her forehead. *This guy?* "Betty Jo? You mean Betty Jo Clark?"

"Of course, that's who I mean. I loved her. We were gonna have a future together." She felt the pressure on the knife tip relax.

"We didn't do anything to Betty Jo," she whispered.

Mike jumped away from her. "Yes, you did. Remember that day the three of you charged her at the bank? Ganged up on her. I heard all about it."

"We confronted her at the bank, yes, but that's where it ended. She was trying to ruin us."

"Ruin you? Betty Jo told me all about your sister Hope. How she was mean to Betty Jo all through high school."

He motioned with the knife for Faith to move to the back of the shop, away from the front window. "Glad you closed the shop and locked the door. Right accomodatin' of you."

Faith took a shaky breath and walked on trembling legs toward the back door. She wondered if she'd die any faster if she vomited her breakfast on the floor. *Dear God, please* . . . .

Grace was just clearing the dining room table when she saw the giant dust ball. Craig Mattheson sped into the Blessing Farm driveway as if it were a Daytona 500 pit. He jumped out of his truck, ran up the porch steps, and banged hard enough to rattle the hinges on the wooden door.

She yanked open the door. Craig? What's the matter? You look like you've seen a ghost."

"I have something to tell you and it ain't all good news."

Grace stepped aside and let him in. With her senses on high alert, her body was as tight as a bow string. "What is it?"

"I'm sure I know who's responsible for the trouble you all been having."

"Who?" Despite her racing pulse, she allowed her face to show nothing but calm. She walked toward the phone that sat on the hallway table.

"It's a guy who drives for me. Name is Mike Reiner."

"You mentioned him the other day. How you figure him? And why would someone who works for you want to put us out of business if you didn't put him up to it?"

"I don't have all the facts yet, but I think Betty Jo was

bank rolling him to do these things. I promised Hope that I'd rehire Mike and his buddy, then we'd try to catch them in the act. I found Richie, but Mike isn't around. I did some snooping in their lockers, then I went back to Richie and threatened to break every bone in his body."

Grace smiled, her hand still resting on the phone. "We'll be bailing you out, too. Breaking into lockers? Threatening people?"

Craig shoved his hands into his pockets. "This is bad, Grace. I provide the locks or my drivers don't drive, so I have access all the time. But Mike's locker wasn't locked and his stuff was still in there, like he has no intention of cleaning it out."

"And that's bad, why?"

"I found notes, instructions from Betty Jo on slashing tires, and stealing your accounts. She promised that boy things she'd never give him unless he helped her."

"Do you think he blew us up too?"

Craig nodded. "He could be capable of that. He's not super bright, but he was always dependable and didn't steal from anyone. I noticed he had a bad temper when he got heated. I didn't find any notes about that, but it makes sense."

"But Betty Jo is dead. She didn't give him orders to blow us up."

"We don't know that. That might have been her last request."

Her legs almost gave out. "Oh, good Lord. And you look like there's more."

"Richie said Mike told him that he was going to teach Merciful something like they'd never seen. Said 'them bitches' had to die."

Grace paled. "I'm calling the Sheriff's office. You tell them what you told me. I'm heading to the salon. Faith and Hope's cutter Dixie are there. If this nut case is heading their way, they need to be warned."

Craig stopped her at the door. "Call the Sheriff from the

car. We're both going."

Faith sat in the chair closest to the bathroom and the back door. First chance she got, she was going through that door and away from this lunatic. *Lord, I know you're listening. I'm scared near to death, but I know you don't want to take me from my family. Help me find a way.*

She sniffed, wiped her eyes and coughed. "Mike, I need to go to the bathroom. I have no idea what time Hope will be back, so I can't wait. Can I go, please?"

He looked at her, then glanced at the bathroom door across the room. He stood, positioned himself in front of the back door, then nodded.

"Thanks," she mumbled. She locked herself in the bathroom and sat on the closed toilet seat. At least she wasn't looking at that damned foldable sword any more. She put her head down and said another prayer. *Why isn't there a window in the damned bathroom?*

Mike banged on the door so hard, she screamed and jumped at the same time. "I'll be out in a minute." She flushed the toilet, then washed her hands and face several times, willing herself to calm down.

He banged on the door again. "Get out here now or I'm coming in."

Faith knew the thin veneer door wouldn't take much to kick in. "I'll be there in a second," she called, hoping she didn't sound nearly as frightened as she was.

She opened the door and stepped out. He pushed her hard and she caught herself by grabbing the arm of a chair. "Take it easy."

"Don't tell me what to do. You'd better get your sister here. I'm not waiting all night for her. I'll just kill you and wait for her to show up. Betty Jo warned me how conniving you all are."

"I still don't understand you and Betty Jo. She usually went after lawyers and business men, not blue-collar guys."

"Me and her was going to get married once we drove you out of Merciful. She knew she couldn't trust your kind any more. She hated you all something fierce, you know. You always thought you was so much better than her, making her life miserable. She just wanted you gone so we could be happy in her town."

"Her town?" Faith straightened her shoulders. Maybe if she told him the truth, he might see how foolish this was. "This town was named by my great-great grandparents. Betty Jo's family's only been here for maybe forty years. If it's anyone's town, it's Hope's town."

He narrowed his eyes. "You quit that. Everything Betty Jo wanted, Hope took away. That ain't fair and you know it." His eyes filled with tears. "And now you took her away from me, too."

Faith didn't dare look away. *Am I faster than he is? Can I be faster than he is so I live to see my kids again? I used to be faster than both Hope and Grace . . . .*

"Mike, nobody in my family had anything to do with Betty Jo's death. We're all real sorry that she ended up like that for sure, but we didn't do it. You kill us, you'd be killing innocent people. You let me walk out the back, you can go out the front."

His laugh sounded like a rusty engine trying to turn over. "No way. I made a promise to Betty Jo and I sure intend to keep it. It's the least I can do, especially now that she's gone. Let's go call your sister." He motioned toward the office door.

Faith struggled to her feet on legs that shook too hard to hold her, just as the back door burst open. When Mike turned, Faith rammed him in the gut with her head, and landed sprawled on top of him on the floor.

She felt the blade of the knife sink deep. *Oh, God, please—*

Chapter Twenty-Two

Broken Circle

Outside the Sheriff's office on a park bench shaded by a tall black oak tree, Hope put her head in her hands and concentrated on her breathing. Jack sat with his hand on her shoulder, but said nothing. She was way past tired. But it didn't matter. She wasn't a quitter and she had two sisters who needed her. She let out a long sigh.

"This is going to be okay, Hope. They have nothing on any of you and the burden of proof is on them."

She raised her head, pushing back hair from her face. "I know. I'm just tired of all this. Thank you for coming, though. I'm sorry I had to pull you away from your other client."

He smiled. "It's okay. At least I wasn't in court and unavailable. None of you ladies should be talking to the authorities without an attorney present. Unless they show up with an arrest warrant, you don't have to go with them. Make them set up an appointment for you to come in. I'll make sure you have council present."

"Okay, thanks. I really need to get back to the shop, though.

Poor Faith and Dixie are probably worried out of their minds, I've been gone so long."

"Then let's get you back to town. Your chariot awaits, Fair Lady." Jack bowed, swept his arm toward his Cadillac ATS, and opened the passenger door for her.

"Oh good, at least I can ride in the front seat going back," she said with a sorry smile.

They drove through Gainesville on State Road 20 until they'd gotten past the University of Florida before Hope spoke again.

"How long have you known Eddie?"

"Probably eighteen, twenty years. He specializes in family law, so I send people his way if they need a good attorney for that stuff."

"And he refers people to you who need criminal law experience."

"Yup. He's a straight shooter. Fair, honest, and in general, makes us criminal lawyers look bad."

His deep laugh made her smile.

"You seem like a pretty straight shooter, too."

"Things are not always what they seem. Remember that."

Hope nodded. She'd remember it okay. Her robust mother struck down by cancer in a year's time. Her healthy father dead at the table without warning. *Eddie's marriage to Betty Jo. Matt's affair . . . .*

"You're right. I'd be smart to keep that in the front of my mind instead of the back. Be a lot less surprises that way."

Jack Edwards drove under the I-75 ramp and continued to highway 41, then on into Merciful. An Alachua County Sheriff's car sped past them with lights and sirens howling, on their way toward Gainesville. Hope shuddered.

"Where to, Hope?"

"Make a right on Main, next corner. Just drop me at the shop. My car's there."

He turned as instructed and stopped in the middle of the street. "What the hell?"

Hope sat straighter. The small street was once again jammed with emergency vehicles, from the ice cream shop down past the salon. "Back up and let's go around to the back. We'll never get though that mess. My sister's in the shop, I've got to get down there, see what's going on, now."

Jack backed up and turned the car around, then made the left past the bank and around the corner. Sheriff's cars and an ambulance stood with lights flashing behind the salon and Erma's building. He parked on the street, directly behind the Post Office.

Oh, please Lord, not Faith. Please let Faith be okay. Hope was out of the car before Jack could lock it. He caught up with her at the ambulance. A big man had her by the arms. A dark haired younger woman and an older woman stood nearby.

"What's going on?" Jack stood next to Hope as he pried Craig's hands from her forearms.

Grace spoke up. "Betty Jo's brainwashed flunky tried to kill Faith while he was waiting for Hope to get back."

"Oh my lord, please tell me she's okay." She looked at Grace who was white as paste. "Grace? Is she okay?"

Grace shook her head. "She's not okay. I don't know how bad she is, but she's not okay."

Jack caught Hope when her knees buckled. "Hang on, Hope. Remember what I said about appearances?"

He peered into her face until she nodded at him. "That's the girl." He turned to watch the responders working in the doorway of the shop, holding Hope close to his side.

She shook her head. "And where's Dixie? Is she okay?" Hope looked around. "Please tell me that they aren't both . . . "

Erma pushed to her side. "Dixie left about two-thirty. That's when I saw the 'Closed' sign on the door, so I walked down to see the reverend." She took Hope's hand in hers. Tears filled her eyes. "I didn't know Faith was still there. The door was locked, so I thought she'd left the shop."

Hope craned her neck to see through the back door and through the massive uniformed shoulders that filled the opening. "You didn't do this, Erma. I'm just glad to know that Dixie's okay." She pulled away from Jack's grasp. "Why in blazes doesn't someone do something?" she shouted.

The shoulders parted and the EMT's came through the doorway with Faith on a gurney, bundled in a blanket, with an oxygen mask on her face. Hope and Grace dashed to her side.

Grace got there first. "Hey, I'm going with you. Hope will be right behind us, okay?" she said. Tears squeezed out of the corner of Faith's closed eyes.

"Ladies, she's got internal bleeding, we've got to get moving." They lifted the gurney into the back of the ambulance and Grace climbed in.

"Where we going?" she hollered to the driver.

"Shands-Gainesville."

Before Hope could say another word, an EMT slammed the doors, checked the latches, then ran to the passenger side of the ambulance. She stood watching the lights flash as they drove down the street.

Dear Lord, please. Please don't take her from us. Take me if you want. She's got the boys. Please, God, please don't let her die.

She shook from head to toe, tears flooding her face, soaking her blouse. Jack pushed a white handkerchief into her clenched fist.

She looked at Craig. She was no longer tired. She was so mad she could barely speak. "I have to get to the hospital. Can you take me to the hospital?" she ground out between clenched teeth.

He looked at his feet, then pointed to his truck. "Let's go sit down, okay? You look like you're about to fall on your face."

"I'm fine. Faith isn't fine, though, and I need to be there. What if she doesn't make it there? I have to go." As she walked in a frantic circle, they formed a protective ring around her.

She looked at each face. "Okay, never mind. My car is out front. I can drive myself."

Jack captured her and put his arm around her shoulders to get her attention. "You are not driving anywhere. The state you're in, you'll kill someone. Maybe even yourself."

"Then you drive. I don't care who the hell drives, just as long as I get there. Why aren't we doing anything?"

"We'll go in a few minutes. They are going to rush her into triage where you can't go anyway. Let's give them time to do what they need to do. I want to know what happened here. It just might impact our case."

Hope sagged against his shoulder, the anger spent, the terrifying thought of her sister dying taking over instead. "I don't care," she sobbed. "I don't care about any of that. Just about Faith . . . "

Craig looked at Jack. "Let's get on the road. I'll fill you in along the way. Hope is breaking my heart."

Aside from Hope's occasional jagged sigh, silence filled Jack's Cadillac once Craig told them what he'd pieced together.

"But why Faith? She didn't have anything to do with this," Hope asked as she brushed away tears for the hundredth time. *God, please don't let her die . . . .*

Hope could barely listen to Craig's retelling without her stomach turning inside out. She gulped for air when he continued.

"When Grace and me busted through the back door, Faith tackled Mike. On the way to the floor, he knifed her. She was conscious the whole time we waited for the ambulance and that's a good sign, Hope."

"Her eyes were closed when they put her in the ambulance, though," Hope whispered.

"Well, I won't lie to you. She probably hurts like hell."

"Where is this guy?" Jack asked Craig.

"Deputies took him out the front door about ten, fifteen minutes ago. He hit his head hard when he hit the floor, but they were haulin' his ass to jail. You probably passed them coming into town."

Jack nodded. "We did. You'd better call Eddie, Hope."

"I will, just let me get my bearings."

Craig leaned forward from the back seat and rested his hand on her shoulder. "Faith's got a lot of grit. She's gonna be fine."

She'd damned well better be. But Hope was out of words. Now it was up to God.

In the silence, it felt like Jack was driving about ten miles an hour. Couldn't he go any faster? Didn't' he understand she had to get to Faith and Grace? And where was Eddie?

She glanced at him, then at the speedometer. *Ten miles over the limit.* She chewed on her bottom lip until it hurt. He doesn't have to do any of this. She leaned her head back against the rest and closed her eyes. She was so tired.

When Faith had been sixteen, she'd been out with a bunch of her high school friends in the State Park that backed onto the Blessing Farm. With only a week until school reopened that August, Hope had told Faith to go have fun, after a summer filled with her Four H projects and the work around the farm.

Daddy was in Ohio, so it was just the girls at home. She and Grace had finished dinner when there was a knock on the front door. It was the Florida Fish and Wildlife Commission officer at the door. Faith and two others had been in an accident in the quarry lake. She was in a coma at the trauma center in Gainesville.

Just remembering that fear made her heart hurt. She opened her eyes and started out at the darkness, wincing at the occasional headlight that glared through the windshield.

Faith had regained consciousness just before midnight, so Hope's prayers for her sister's recovery were answered. But she'd never forget the heartbreaking sobs of the parents of the other child who would never regain consciousness again.

"Maybe you should try Eddie again," Jack said softly. His words rescued Hope from her dark thoughts.

"Okay." She pulled her cell phone from the pocket on herpurse and pressed redial.

When he answered, it was all she could do to talk around the lump in her throat.

She glanced at Jack and listened to Eddie's questions. "I've been with Jack all day, actually. I was at the sheriff's office for hours and hours. When Jack drove me back to the shop, we found every emergency responder within fifty miles at the salon. Faith was stabbed. I don't know how bad it is."

Again, she listened, her head pounding. "That's fine." Then, "No, they didn't arrest me. Doesn't matter. I just wanted you to know what was going on. We're all going to be at Shands."

Eddie spoke, then without a word, Hope closed the phone. "He's going to meet us there as soon as he can. Said he can get out of Ocala in another ten minutes or so. That will put him at the hospital in about forty-five minutes."

"I'm beginning to think this Betty Jo wasn't playing with a full deck," Jack said as he turned into the hospital parking lot.

"She wasn't. Never was, I guess. But this is just too strange. I wonder if she was just using Mike, or was she really so twisted she genuinely thought I was her enemy?"

Craig cleared his throat. "I don't know. Those notes were pretty unnerving. People tell the same lies so often they begin to believe the lies are the truth. I wasn't married to her long, but Betty Jo could really make things look the way she wanted to."

Jack parked the car. They got out and walked toward

the Emergency entrance. "You're right. Not the case with a psychopath, but it can be with a sociopath. It's pretty clear she was having some mental challenges."

Hope didn't care about Betty Jo or her issues. "If Faith doesn't make it, I'm going to wish I *did* kill Betty Jo," she said, fighting back the tears once again. *God, please* . . . .

The two men flanked her. Craig held the door open and they moved toward the registration desk.

"And I could probably get a not guilty verdict for it, too ," said Jack. "But you didn't, and Faith is going to all right, I'm sure. Let's go find your sisters."

Eddie was finishing the deposition of a battered young woman seeking a divorce from her bully of a husband when Hope's call had come in.

"Sarah, would you call Mrs. Richardson a cab, please? I've got an emergency in Gainesville to take care of."

"Sure, Mr. Highspring. Be glad to." The receptionist was twenty-three and had plans to be a lawyer herself one day. He smiled at her.

"Once she's safely on her way, you lock up and go home. I'll see you Monday. We don't have court or appointments tomorrow and we've put in some late hours this week. You have a great weekend."

She was still thanking him while he stuffed file folders and his laptop into the case. "Don't forget to lock up," he reminded her as he headed out the door.

His car was in the parking garage beneath the building, but it seemed to take forever before he was driving the two blocks to get to I-75. He'd be in Gainesville in less than an hour if the traffic was moving without a problem.

He gave the OnStar Shawn Jackson's home number and waited while the metallic clicks and rings filled the car. On the fifth ring, Shawn answered the phone.

"Eddie? How are you?"

"I'm doing fine, Shawn, thanks. How are you doing today? Headaches better?"

"They are. Keep falling over when I stand up, but Mrs. Higgins loaned me her late husband's walker and I'm more stable with that."

"Good, good, Shawn. Glad to hear you're getting better. It's going to take time, but you'll get it all back. Have you remembered any more about the weekend you were attacked?"

The air was quiet except for the air conditioning fan. "Shawn? Still there?"

He heard a sigh. "Yes, I'm here. And yes, I'm getting bits and pieces of things that I haven't put together yet. They're strange things. Is it important?"

Eddie took a breath and decided on a gamble. "They could be, Shawn. Hope was picked up this morning for the murder of Betty Jo. You and I both know she didn't do it."

"Oh lord, no. Of course she didn't do it. But do we know who did? I mean how can I help with this? Is it the same person who hit me?"

"I don't know, I really don't know. Have you heard anything about your car yet? Have they found it? We know you left for the lake in it, but your car wasn't found there. Were you carjacked, maybe?"

Again, silence filled the car. "I . . . I don't think so. I remember getting into someone else's car. Hardware store. I dreamed about a hardware store with a bait sign in the window. But I don't know where it is or why I dreamed about it."

"You've been fishing at Orange Lake for years. Don't you always stop at the same place for your license and bait and stuff?"

"I do. But this store isn't familiar. And Eddie?"

"Yeah?"

"I keep seeing Betty Jo tied to a chair. She isn't hurt, just tied to a chair. Did the police find her car?"

He hated where this was taking his friend, but he needed to know the truth. "Yes, they did. Found it not a half mile from the dock where you were discovered."

"That's odd, isn't it?" Shawn said softly as though speaking to himself rather than his attorney.

"Shawn, do you remember where you spent your eighteenth birthday, by any chance?"

This time Eddie could hear Shawn Jackson's tears. "Yes, I do. And you wouldn't be asking if you didn't already know the answer."

"Shawn?" Eddie pressed.

"I was in Eastman, Georgia. At the Prison for Youthful Offenders."

Hope sat in the emergency surgical waiting room and watched as Grace paced the floor. Watching Grace distracted her from her thoughts. What would she do if Faith didn't make it? What about her boys? Would they ever forgive her? Could she ever forgive herself?

Craig watched Grace, too, his hands clasped tightly in front of him as he sat on the tired orange sofa. After a brief hug when they'd arrived, he'd let her go and she'd done twenty miles on those black and white tiles. Jack had gotten a call and left with a promise to check in every couple of hours to see if they needed anything.

Just about paralyzed with fatigue and worry, Hope envied the energy that kept her sister pacing back and forth from the sofa to the windows and back. The vanilla-laced antiseptic smell of the hospital made her wrinkle her nose. The sunny yellow walls kept the despair and fear at the outer fringes of her mind.

"How long does this shit take?" Grace asked for the third time in an hour.

"I have no idea. They'll come get us when they take her to recovery." Hope forced herself to her feet. "I'm going down the hall for a cup of coffee. Do you want one?"

Grace shook her head and dropped onto the sofa. "Another cup of coffee and you'll be prying me off the ceiling. What I really need is a drink."

Craig pushed himself to his feet. "Well, as soon as we know Faith is okay, we'll go to the hotel and get that drink. Several if we want them. I'm buying."

Grace sent him a worn smile and he walked to her side. "Any chance you could eat something? They've got to have food around here."

"No. Hell, maybe. I've got such a headache I can barely think. What time is it?"

Hope glanced at her cell phone. "Almost seven. Craig's right, we probably should get a snack—try to eat something. We won't be any good to anyone if we fall on our faces, right?"

"Guess you're right. I'm going to check at the nursing station first."

They walked to the desk and were again told that Faith was still in surgery. "Want to take the stairs?" Grace asked Hope. Craig stayed behind them like a sentinel.

"Sure. It's only a few floors and I can use a good stretch."

They descended in silence. Hope said a prayer with each step. *Thank you for saving my sisters. Thank you for saving Faith.*

Craig pulled open the door on the first floor and held it for the women. "Slowing down, sis?" Grace said.

"Yes, in case you haven't realized, I'm not all that short of sixty, kiddo. And stairs aren't in my daily workout routine."

"Do *you* have a daily workout routine?" Grace said with a grimace.

"Hell no. Who the heck has time for exercise?"

Craig walked beside them, his arm around Grace's shoulder.

"You look like you're in fine shape. Both of you."

They shuffled into the cafeteria, picked up a tray and moved slowly along the counters and coolers. "Nothing looks appealing, does it?" Grace frowned.

"We're too emotional. Grab a couple of orange juices and bananas. I don't see much left worth eating."

Craig paid the cashier but before they could take two steps, Hope's phone rang. Faith was out of surgery and on her way to recovery.

"Let's go." Grace gulped the orange juice from the carton, and tossed it into the trash can. Craig stood holding the tray, looking from Hope to Grace.

Hope had collapsed into a chair. "Doctor will see us in thirty minutes. He wants to clean up first. Just sit down and eat your banana."

"I'm too old for you to mother anymore, Hope. I'm going up, you coming?"

"I'll be there in a few minutes. I want to find out what's taking Eddie so long."

Grace sighed and looked at Craig who didn't look inclined to move, either. "Fine. I'm going outside on the patio for some air. I'll be back in a few minutes."

"Sure. I'll be right here." *Trying to keep what's left of my sanity from unraveling . . . .*

The surgeon, a heavy-set man in his late forties with black hair and high cheekbones, stood facing the trio, his hands in the pockets of his white hospital coat.

"Your sister is a lucky woman. The wound was serious and she's now going to be operating on one kidney, but she's healthy and I think she'll do just fine. She'll be with us for a week so we can be sure she doesn't develop an infection."

"Will she need anything special when she goes home?" Hope asked.

He smiled. "She won't want to do stairs for a few weeks, but she should get regular exercise. Low fat diet would be best on her system. In six months, she'll feel like new."

Hope's knees almost gave out and she gave up keeping back the tears. *Thank you, thank you, thank you, Lord.* She smiled at Craig when he steadied her by grabbing her by the arm.

"Can we go see her? We won't stay long, we just want to see her. Let her know we're here," said Hope.

"You can go down and take a look through the window, but I don't want her having visitors tonight. Let's get the antibiotics going overnight and you can see her in the morning. I've sedated her and she's not going to wake up until then. Just give the nurses a few minutes to get her settled into the ICU, okay?"

All questions answered, the doctor walked down the hall and left them sitting in the waiting room.

"Did you reach Eddie?" Grace asked as she thumbed through the old National Geographic again.

Hope shook her head. "No, it went straight to voice mail. I just left him a message. I sure hope nothing's happened to him, now."

"I'm sure he's fine, sis. He'll be here as soon as he can," said Grace. They sat in silence. The minutes dragged on forever before the nurse signaled for them to follow her.

Arm in arm, Hope and Grace walked to the ICU window. They watched the nurses finish setting up the monitors and IV bags attached to Faith. She never moved. When the sheets were neatly pulled up to her chin and the privacy curtain pulled around, they took their cue to leave.

"Goodnight, little sister," Hope and Grace said in unison. Craig took Grace's hand.

They headed for the elevator. Grace put her arm around Hope's shoulder and squeezed before she let go. Then she stabbed the down arrow with her index finger.

Hope watched as Craig pulled Grace into his arms and closed his eyes. *He seems like a good man and Grace would be happy with a good man . . . .*

The elevator doors opened, and Hope stepped inside. "Let's go get that drink.

The threesome walked the block and a half to the Hyatt where Jack had made reservations for them to stay. Craig held the door for Grace and Hope. Just as the door closed, *The Saints Go Marching In* played from Hope's shirt pocket. She pulled it out, glanced at the number and flipped it open.

"We've just left the hospital. Where are you?" She frowned as she listened to his reply. "Okay, talk to you later."

"Something wrong?" Grace asked.

"I really don't know. But Eddie's heading for Merciful. Said he has to talk to Shawn Jackson—tonight."

Chapter Twenty-Three

Hidden Truths

Eddie pulled into the rectory driveway a little after nine. He parked, climbed out and leaned against the car. He folded his arms and stared at the rectory for a long moment. *Hope may never forgive me for not being at the hospital, but if I don't unravel this mess fast, she might be headed for jail. And what deep dark secret is my friend here hiding?*

He pushed himself off the car, marched up the porch steps, and knocked on the door.

Margaret Ann opened the door. "Well, what are you doing here? Have you heard from Hope? How is Faith doing?"

He was too tired to smile but he tried anyway. "I really need to talk to the reverend. Hope said Faith is resting, and she's going to be fine in time. I'm sure she'll call you later or first thing in the morning. It's been a long day for everyone."

Margaret Ann nodded. "Praise God," she said with a wide grin. "Hope doesn't need any more grief than she's already got." She pointed toward the doorway. "He's in the front parlor watching television. Want some coffee?"

"I'd love a cup. Thanks."

Eddie found Sean sitting in a taupe leather chair, staring at a program on the History Channel. "Shawn, how are you doing?"

"Eddie? What brings you here so late?"

Margaret Ann entered the room and set a tray of coffee and cookies on the round table separating the two chairs. "If you don't need anything else, I'll say goodnight."

"Thanks, Margaret Ann," Eddie said.

"Yes, thank you for all your good care. Goodnight," said Shawn.

Eddie sipped his coffee and stared at the muted television. "I'm sorry, but I can't let this go. I think we have some talking to do." *And if I don't get the right answers, I might just finish what someone else started with you, buddy.* He took another sip to calm down.

Shawn nodded. "Yes, I guess we do. First, tell me how Hope is holding up."

Eddie placed his mug on the tray. "How the hell do you *think* she's doing? Before a madman almost killed her sister, she spent all day at the Sheriff's office answering questions about a murder she didn't commit. We both know she's innocent. Don't we?" Eddie could feel his blood pressure rising. He forced himself to put on his poker face and wait.

"She's innocent," Shawn whispered after a long silence.

Damned right, she is! Eddie opened his briefcase, pulled papers from a manila envelope and laid them on Shawn's lap.

The reverend scanned the documents, and looked up at Eddie. "Where did you get these?"

"The first time I saw the clipping was with your belongings at the hospital. I was curious about why you had it. So I did a little digging." He inched forward to the edge of the chair and perched like a cat waiting for a mouse.

"What are you going to do with the information?"

Eddie relaxed back into the chair. "Why don't you fill in the blanks for me, Shawn?"

"This all happened a long time ago. I was a kid. Just turned sixteen, a new driver."

Eddie softened his voice. "How did you get involved in a mess like that?"

Shawn buried his face in his hands, and wiped away tears. "My father died in a car accident when I was fourteen. I had three younger brothers and a baby sister. I became the man of the house.

"Dad was a construction worker. He was in and out of work, you know how that is. When he got in the accident, he had no insurance and left us flat broke with nothing but bills."

He struggled to his feet and steadied himself on the arm of the chair. "I'm going to have a touch of whiskey. Would you like to join me?"

Eddie nodded. "I'm up for that. Why not?"

Shawn poured a drink for Eddie and one for himself. He took a hefty swig and carried the drinks back to his chair. "Mom cleaned houses, and took in ironing, anything to stay off the welfare list. She sold our house and bought a trailer."

"Did you grow up in Atlanta?" Eddie asked.

Shawn shook his head. "No. The trailer park was on the outskirts of the city. The poor side of Fulton County.

"I did odd jobs. I delivered newspapers, raked leaves, mowed lawns, bagged groceries. But it seemed we never had enough money to cover our expenses. So, one day, a guy I knew asked me if I wanted to make a lot of money for a little bit of work. All I had to do was drive a car."

"You must have known there was something wrong wih that," Eddie said quietly.

Shawn shrugged. "You have no idea how hard life was back then. Five kids to buy clothes and food for. No money for medicines or doctors or haircuts. My mother worked herself to death and we never had enough. So, when a few of the guys I hung out with said they were going to rob a bank, I figured if I didn't go inside the bank, it'd be okay."

He took a swallow of the whiskey and let it burn at the back of his throat. "I'm proud of who I've become since. I'm a good minister, and I've come a long way from that confused kid. I had good friends in Percy Blessing and you. I thought the past was buried for good." He stared into the glass and sighed. "Our friendship will probably come to a screeching halt when you hear the rest of my story."

Are you out of your mind? Eddie stared Shawn square in the eye. "Our friendship is definitely over if you don't tell me the truth and help clear Hope."

"I understand. I want to help Hope, too." He inhaled a huge breath and sighed. "I had my driver's license, and I delivered groceries for a small local market. I used their beat-up old station wagon to make the deliveries."

Eddie nodded. "The perfect getaway car?"

Shawn nodded. "Something like that. Anyhow, the guys thought we would never get caught. They wore ski masks to do the robbery. I kept the car running. When the guys brought the money back to the car, I froze." Shawn clenched his fists. "They started yelling at me, but I couldn't move."

"What happened next?"

"I panicked." Shawn waved his right hand in a circular fashion. "I put the pedal to the metal and zoomed down the street speeding until . . . ." Shawn choked up. "Until I ran up the curb and..." Shawn covered his face and wept.

"And hit the nine-year-old boy outside the laundromat," Eddie finished.

"Yes." Shawn trembled. "I struck and killed a child with the getaway car in an armed bank robbery."

Shawn sat for several minutes with his head buried in his hands. Eddie patted his shoulder. "I know this is tough. I appreciate your honesty. How were you charged?"

Shawn lifted his head. "I was charged with vehicular manslaughter in a plea deal to testify against the others. I promised my mother that I'd try to make it right, but I'll never forget the look of grief and despair on that boy's mother's face."

Eddie got to his feet and walked to the window. He stared into the darkness. "What does any of this have to do with Betty Jo?" he asked.

"She didn't like me helping Hope and her sisters. Her goal in life was to ruin Hope Blessing and her family any way she could."

Eddie moved his head from side to side. "How well I know that, brother. How well I know that. Was she blackmailing you?"

"That was her plan." Shawn sat straighter in his chair. "She had a private detective investigate my past until he found something."

Eddie waved palms up. "She sure had the money and the resources to do so."

"I was on my way to the cabin to fish, because all this fussing, and losing Percy was weighing me down. When I came out of the Quicki-Mart, she was parked behind me. I told her to get lost and do whatever she had to do to me, 'cause I paid my time, but to leave Hope alone. She said if I wasn't gonna listen to her, the Blessing girls would really pay."

Shawn took Eddie's empty glass and poured two more whiskeys. "So, I drove my car to the bait store just outside Orange Lake and bought my license and bait, but she was still sitting there, parked beside me. So, I got in her car, figuring to talk some sense into her. She started driving."

"Well, that explains why they didn't find your car at the lake."

"I had Betty Jo drive us to the cabin so we could talk. I thought I could calm her down and reason with her. When we got to the cabin, she yelled and screamed about Hope. She said she would ruin me, Hope, and you, too if I didn't play along with her. She got hysterical, yellin', and cussin'. Then she started punching and hitting me. So, I grabbed her arms behind her, took off my belt and tied her to the kitchen chair."

"When she was mad, she could do a lot of damage. That's something I'll never forget." Eddie raised his glass in a mock salute. *A whole lot of damage.*

"Eddie, you have to believe me, I've never been mean or treated a woman bad like that in my life. But Betty Jo went crazy like a gator that hadn't eaten in a week."

"I know those tantrums of Betty Jo's all too well, my friend. All too well."

"I went for a walk to do some praying. Hoping she would be calmer, and then I would untie her. When I got back into the cabin, she was gone. I called out her name, ran all around the outside of the cabin trying to find her, and then whack. She came up behind me and banged me in the side of the head with something. We were on the dock. I was dizzy, then she hit me again, and I couldn't even see. I grabbed at her to keep from falling in the lake. After that I don't remember. Could she have fallen in?"

"Could be. Betty Jo couldn't swim," Eddie said. "I had a boat years ago when we were together, but she would never go out in it with me. She was terrified of the water."

"I never knew she was afraid of anything," Shawn said.

"She was afraid of everything, she just wouldn't show it. I'm betting she drowned accidently. Some fisherman rescued you."

"I don't know what happened. After she hit me the second time, I was about done."

"You still want to help Hope, don't you?"

"I'll do anything to help her out."

Eddie stood. "Well, you know what you have to do then."

"Can you give me a ride to the Sheriff's office? I'd rather they didn't come out here to the church."

Chapter Twenty-Four

Percy's Girls

Hope sat across from her sisters at the dining room table in the rehab center, unable to keep the smile off her face. Faith still had a ways to go, but she was improving daily and they hoped to have her home in a matter of weeks.

Hope put toast and eggs on her sister's plate. "How are you feeling today?"

"Great." Faith raised her teacup in the air. "I feel like I'm the luckiest woman in Florida to be sitting here alive."

Grace patted her twin sister's hand. "Amen, sister. That beauty shop catastrophe could have ended much worse. But please explain to me, *why* you decided to tackle the guy. That's not really your style."

"It may not have been my style when we were growing up, but when you have two rambunctious boys, you learn how effective a tackle can be."

"Probably would have been better for you if the guy hadn't outweighed you by a hundred pounds, but, well, all I can say is that I'm glad you're okay." Grace picked up the last piece of bacon and chomped on it.

"Did you talk to the boys yet? Will they be here for your homecoming party?" Hope asked.

"They said they'd call me later on today. Their grandparents are taking them to see fireworks after dinner, so we'll talk before then."

Grace looked at Hope. "Is Shawn coming to the barbeque tonight?"

"I talked with him yesterday morning. He and Mrs. Higgins were making potato salad to bring along, so I'm expecting him."

Faith shook her head. "That's just the saddest thing, isn't it? Betty Jo was going to ruin him for being our friend and now he'll probably go to jail even though she tried to kill him."

Grace laughed. "She tried to kill him because he restrained her. But he didn't force her to go there, and he didn't hurt her, so maybe he'll get off with probation or something. What the hell were the charges, anyway?"

"Jack Edward's got them reduced to unlawful imprisonment. He's pretty optimistic that the good Reverend is going to be just fine." Hope reached for the pitcher of orange juice. "And if prayers count, I *know* he will be."

"Well, I'm living proof that prayers count," said Faith.

Grace's cell phone buzzed, alerting her to an incoming text message. She glanced at the message and smiled.

"That smile tells me the message is from Craig," Faith teased.

Grace grinned. "He said he'll be at the farm at six with a watermelon."

"So, which one is it going to be, Grace? Uncle Sam or Craig?" Hope winked.

"I've definitely decided to get out, and that's going to take at least six months, but by end of the year, I'll be a full-fledged civilian." Grace wiped her mouth with a napkin and pushed her chair away from the table. "As for Craig, that remains to be seen."

Faith giggled. "From what I've seen, that man will be more than willing to put up with any engineering *you'd* like to do."

Grace stacked her dishes and shot her sister a look.

"What time is Eddie coming to show us Daddy's second CD?" Faith asked Hope.

"I told him to come at eleven-thirty, that way we can view the CD, discuss whatever Daddy has to say, and still have time to get back to the farm to set up for the barbeque."

"Sounds like a plan." Faith struggled to her feet. She looked at Grace. "Did you ever play the CD Daddy left for you?"

Grace looked out the window, then at the floor. "No, I started to more than once, but then everything happened, and I just didn't get back to it." She looked at Faith. "Did you?"

Faith shook her head. "No, me either. When Isiah broke his leg, I left it at the house and never did get back to it."

Both girls looked at Hope. She stared back at them. "Well, I got through part of mine, but not the whole thing."

"And?" Grace and Faith asked in unison.

"And, he told me to trust you and let you go. Told me he was sorry for putting me in a tough position. That was about all I could take."

Grace put her hands on Faith's walker. "He's right you know. You can trust us to do the right things. You raised us good, Hope."

She fought the tears and tried to clear the lump in her throat with a cough. "Why don't you and Faith walk down to the rose garden and back like the doctor ordered?" Hope gathered dishes from the table. "I'll meet you back in your room."

"I could get used to this." Faith smiled as she pushed her walker through the dining room doorway.

Once again, the three sisters gathered with Eddie to view the final portion of their father's video will. They were in Faith's room at the rehab center and the door was closed with a Do

Not Disturb sign on the outside.

Eddie looked at each woman and nodded. "Are you ready?"

They looked at each other. Hope answered. "We're ready as we'll ever be."

The CD clicked and whirled and then Percy Blessing's face appeared on the computer screen.

Well girls, I'm very proud of you. Eddie had instructions not to show this to you unless you were still together, working as a team. I know things haven't been easy because I didn't leave you much to work with, but knowing God and knowing you, I'm sure it's under control.

What I wanted to say to you now is that I don't care about the trucking company or even the farm for that matter. If you have to give up on them, you have my permission to do that. But you don't ever give up on each other or yourselves. You're bright, beautiful women and I'm proud that you are my daughters. Take care and know how much I love you.

The girls dabbed at their eyes with tissues. Eddie removed the CD, and shut down his computer. "Your father's insurance check arrived, and I have money for you. It should help things considerably."

He handed Grace the check. She glanced at it and then looked at him. "This is for $75,000. You were supposed to recoup your fees from this."

Eddie looked at Hope. "This family doesn't owe me anything."

Faith and Grace thanked him. Then he looked at Hope. "Can I talk to you a moment, outside?" She nodded, then followed him out into the hall, closing Faith's door behind her.

"Are you okay?" he asked.

She looked up at him. "I'm all right, I guess. Thank you for all you've done for us. I suspect this probably wasn't easy for you, either."

He reached for her hand. "I know we haven't talked in almost a week, but how about you and me? Are we okay?"

"Define 'okay.'" She left her hand in his.

"Hmm." Eddie rubbed his chin. "Well, I guess what I'm really asking is do you still hate me or am I invited to the barbeque?"

Hope laughed and then kissed his cheek.

Eddie felt the heat rise in his face. "Lord, it feels good to hear you really laugh again".

"I don't hate you, and yes you're invited to the barbeque." She stood on the tips of her toes and pressed close to his ear.

"And who knows," she whispered, "maybe you'll be invited to some *other* things, too."

Be my rock and refuge, my secure stronghold;
for you are my rock and fortress.
My god, rescue me from the power of the wicked,
from the clutches of the violent.
You are my hope, Lord; my trust, God, from my youth.
Psalm 72:3-5

About The Authors

Daria Ludas w/a D.K. Ludas

Daria has always enjoyed reading and writing. At the age of ten she received a small typewriter for Christmas. She quickly typed several copies of a neighborhood newspaper called "The Linford Ledger," which was named for the development she lived in. She graduated from the Nancy Drew Mysteries to A Summer Place in sixth grade, without her parent's knowledge. She then read Agatha Christie mysteries (Miss Marple a favorite). She currently reads Lisa Scottoline and Robert Parker.

Daria is a retired elementary school teacher, and is currently a New Jersey Realtor. She has been published in short fiction since 2005. When not writing or selling homes, she is involved in town politics, church organizations, Liberty States Fiction Writers and Sisters in Crime. She lives in New Jersey with her husband, Gary and daughter, Jennie who are both supportive of her writing.

About The Authors

Nancy Quatrano w/a N.L. Quatrano

Nancy's been writing since around the age of 13. She was sure she would die when her first crush went home after summer vacation where they met on the Great Lakes. Born and raised in New Jersey, her poems became song lyrics when she learned to play guitar. Her passion for mysteries started with Nancy Drew and Hardy Boy books, blossomed with Agatha Christie and Edgar Allen Poe, and then grew into a love for Sue Grafton, Robert B. Parker and Elmore Leonard, to name her favorites. She's been published since 1999 in short fiction and currently has a mystery series in publication as well, writing as N.L. Quatrano. She's a neighborhood columnist for the St. Augustine Record where her column is published semi-monthly. When she's not working with Rotary, the town empowerment group, or her church, she does content editing, copy writing, and press releases at her business, On-Target Words. And in her spare time, she writes her novels. She says that her two long-time feline companions help her work the late nights to keep her fiction writing going. Her website is NLQuatrano.com and her email is Nancy@NLQuatrano.com

Made in the USA
Middletown, DE
16 March 2019